BETWEEN MOONS

LILLY CAIN

Work has been the focus of Helen Mathews' life for the last seven years. Determined to prove her father wrong, and that she is as good or better than a son would have been, Helen has sacrificed her personal life to make it to the top in her land development company. But putting the projects before friendship and love hasn't been easy. Even when the project is as good for the community as a hospital, there are always losses.

David Sherman is good at winning. He's built his company from the ground up and is ready to play with the big boys. Or big girls, in the case of his newest development. Helen and her company are the perfect partners for his current project. She has the drive and the power he needs. If only she'd stay put and stop disappearing on him. Something is wrong and if there is one thing he can't resist, it's a puzzle. Or a weeping woman.

When a Gypsy curse interrupts a life devoted to work, Helen must find a balance between the wilderness and the board-room. But is there a chance for balance when David charges to the rescue? One thing for sure, Helen is no damsel in distress.

Between Moons

Lilly Cain

ISBN 9781775212058

Cover design by Candace Phillips Gilmer
Flirtation Designs

Discover other titles by Lilly Cain www.lillycain.com

To my family, Emma and Katherine especially, who are more patient than I am. And to my writing friends, Sara, Renee, Cathy, and Donna, who push me to do more. Thank you for being there.

"We'd like to congratulate Ms. Mathews on her recent closure of the largest deal this firm has seen in ten years. Raise your glasses and toast our sharpest nose for business, our shark in these shallow market waters, Ms. Helen Mathews!"

It was a perfect moment. The entire company had gathered to celebrate her promotion to partner, something she'd worked toward for the last few years with little time for anything else. She had the full attention of the company owner. She looked fantastic, and the room was filled with white linen-draped tables topped with crystal and candles. The food was picture perfect, even if she couldn't bring herself to taste it. Her stomach twisted as she waited for his toast to continue and the announcement to be made.

Henry Winfield, President of Multoma, raised his glass of champagne and smiled at the gathered executives at the head table. In turn, they raised their glasses and smiled, although to most observers it probably looked more like the baring of teeth in a pack of wolves, with none willing to show a moment's weakness.

As Helen rose to accept her accolades, a disturbance at the back of the room drew the focus away from her and toward a small group of people. Two young men dressed in jeans and leather jackets pushed their way through the employees gathered in the hotel convention room, making way for an older woman. They rushed to reach the head table where Helen stood and the Board of Directors of Multoma Development International sat.

As they approached, the two men flanked the oddly dressed older woman. She seemed familiar, but Helen couldn't quite place her. A long, full skirt fell to her ankles, with a ruby scarf providing a brilliant splash of color between the skirt and her white blouse. She was weighted down with rings on every finger. Her hair was gray, but she wore it simply pulled back from her face, the long waves falling past her shoulders. Her black eyes flashed at Helen, and her sneering smile was cold.

"Ms. Mathews." The old woman spoke, her clear voice belying any trace of age and certainly reaching all the corners of the room. "It is good to see that you're being recognized as the shark that you are—a predator that would eat its own young."

A collective gasp rippled through the room. Helen sucked in a breath, and lifted her chin in indignation. Heat rushed to her face and she could imagine the redness creeping toward her neckline when she heard a few tittering laughs some-where toward the back of the gathering. Annoyance had her gritting her teeth as she struggled to produce her usual professional smile. Already there were motions indicating that security had been called, so Helen remained standing, facing the odd group.

"Many thanks for the compliment." Helen controlled her voice to reflect only sarcasm, her intonation poisonous. "An insult so strong must indicate that I've moved up in the ranks of my critics' black list. However, now is not the time to trade respects. Perhaps you could reach me at the office for an appointment."

"I don't think so. We've had our meetings, and you've still ignored our claim to our rightful land. We don't ask for much. We rarely stay in one place, but still, we must have those few places where we can meet and be ourselves. The Rom will always be travelers, but you have taken away one of our last refuges."

As the old woman spoke, Helen suddenly realized who the person before her was. This was the same well-dressed, professional lawyer she'd been meeting with over a land dispute, a dispute involving the very deal she was being recognized for. Bianca Donceanu's people were the Rom—a branch of American Romanians that retained their wandering Gypsy ways. They'd fought to keep the land—said it was their right to camp there annually as they had for generations—when in truth, the land belonged only to the government.

Sounds of approaching security personnel could be heard, and the woman glared hard at Helen and stroked a long, golden chain hanging about her neck. Her voice became more heavily accented, her phrasing more formal. "I curse you now, Helen Mathews. I curse you in the way of my people. I curse you three times as one who devours, as one who bares her fangs against those who would keep their own, and as the predator you truly are."

With a flick of her wrist the Rom woman reached into some hidden pocket within her skirts and pulled out a small bottle. In a fluid motion she flung it toward Helen. Helen stepped back but the tiny flask smashed against the table in front of her, splashing its contents out and upward, spattering Helen from head to toe.

By now, the old woman was shouting, racing to finish the

words she now spoke in a foreign tongue before the guards dragged the uninvited accusers from the room. Helen stood frozen, caught in the spell of the Rom curse. She suppressed the urge to shiver, her blood running cold. She brushed her fingers over the flecks of liquid on her cheek. Everyone near her stared in hushed shock, even Mr. Winfield, a man she'd never seen off-pace.

She looked down at her hand and realized she was covered in blood.

1

"Well, where the hell is she?" David Sherman's voice carried his annoyance clearly to the receptionist on the other end of the telephone. "I've been trying to reach Ms. Mathews all week. Does she *not* want to close this deal? There are at least two other companies I could go to with this. Understand?"

"I'm sorry, Mr. Sherman. Ms. Mathews will be returning to the office tomorrow. I'm sure she'll contact you right away."

"She'd better. We can't sit on this for much longer."

David hung up the phone and raised a hand to his aching head. What had he been thinking of, convincing himself that this woman was the only one for the job? That she was the only one who could make or break this deal? She'd been vague in her replies to his calls early last week, although she'd confirmed that the deal was one Multoma would be interested in. Then she'd simply disappeared. For God's sake, they hadn't even met yet.

Her secretary couldn't even say where she was. Couldn't or wouldn't. David tensed as the thought occurred to him again that perhaps she had taken the idea he'd brought to the table and offered it to another firm. She was, after all, reputed to be absolutely ruthless. Since her apparent desertion after their last discussion, her absence was all he could think about.

David leaned back into his black leather chair, reclining as he considered the very real possibility of a double-cross. He had put together a tasty package of land just waiting for a big enough developer, and a plan to create a new retail and office center in Philadelphia. Would she steal that idea? He ran frustrated fingers though his hair.

She might. It was time to meet the woman in person. Time to get a better feel for her ethics. It was well known that she was strong, smart, and one of the best negotiators in the trade. She'd won concessions for developments from both the government and the public that no one had thought possible. It was because of her that several unused and derelict sections of land, reclaimed from what used to be one of Detroit's largest dumps, were now being developed successfully into a huge science center and hospital. She'd been recognized by her company and made a senior partner, a feat practically unheard of for so young a woman in this field.

David leaned forward and pressed the intercom button to summon his secretary. He looked around his spacious office. He was no small-time operator; he could take on Helen Mathews. If she thought she could get away with stealing the biggest development he'd ever cultivated, she could think again. His corner office with a view in the largest office building in Philadelphia was proof of that.

Sally, his assistant, entered the room quietly. For a moment David admired her. She was just his type: blond, curvy, and willing. And yet, there just wasn't any pull, any excitement, any challenge. Beyond that, he would simply never get involved with someone he worked with. He had more than enough proof that that path led to certain disaster.

"Can I help you, Mr. Sherman?" She paused in front of his desk, and leaned just a tad too far over, David noted. Although he certainly took a moment to admire the proffered view of her breasts, he was familiar with the pose. Women considered him handsome, but it was the power and money he controlled that seemed to be the deciding factor in their interest. Women loved power. It would be nice if someone wanted him for once, not just the money and prestige that came with his lifestyle.

"I need travel arrangements to New York, Sally." David drew her attention back to work. Once, the kind of challenge she was silently offering would have aroused him, co-worker or not. He had to face it—he wasn't interested, and it wasn't because she worked for him. She was much the same as the last three women he'd had affairs with, he couldn't bring himself to start the cycle again.

She straightened immediately and smoothed her skirt with ill-concealed irritation. He ignored it, but what else could he do but pretend her silent offer had never happened?

"I want the next flight available. Book me first class and make reservations for dinner at Ruby Foo's, in a private dining room. I'll be bringing a business prospect, so be sure we get it, no matter what we have to shell out. I'll stay at my apartment, so you know where to contact me."

David rattled off several more instructions and left a list of reports he wanted generated and sent to him in New York. Within a few moments he was on his way out the door. It only occurred to him then that he hadn't soothed Sally's bruised ego. A quick cell call and an offer of the day off while he was gone was all it took. He could only hope that it would go as well with Helen Mathews.

Helen collapsed with exhaustion into her office chair. Any brief time away from her desk meant a huge pile of catch-up work, no matter how necessary the absence. Nearly a week off for the third time in as many months had left her with an avalanche of paperwork and her secretary and receptionist both looked at her as if she'd abandoned them. She simply could not explain to them why she'd left or where she'd gone.

Only their longtime loyalty kept them from asking too many questions. The two women had risen with her through the ranks of Multoma Developments and knew they owed her for the opportunities they had been given. Not one word had been said, at least not by them, not even when she knew they noticed a change in her appearance as well as habits.

Helen dug through the pile of papers left on her 'in' tray and sifted out the most important of the reports she'd requested before she left. How much longer could she keep this up? Surely, it wouldn't be long before someone higher up noted her absences. She pulled out the numbers on David Sherman's proposal. She'd only had time to skim it before she'd left last week. It was an excellent plan, one that combined land once considered unusable and therefore cheap, and an innovative architectural concept for engineering office space over what was basically a swamp.

She'd pulled all the information Multoma had on Sherman's past operations and on the man himself, and had taken it away with her. There were times when she'd been able to read during her absence, although deciphering numbers proved impossible. Something about the way she processed information around the time of the full moon was very different. There was a lot to review. He'd been a busy man over the last couple of years, and she discovered his ideas had proved quite interesting and profitable for Multoma before, although her personal team had never worked with him.

As for the man, she'd Googled him and found more than she expected. According to the press, he'd never been married, had worked at the same firm until he became full partner, and was a serious contributor to various charities, including wildlife preservation. And yet, he was a hunter, well proven in his skill against wild game. He owned several apartments and condos across the country.

It was too bad she'd angered him by not contacting him last week. Her receptionist told her how irritated he'd been on the phone when he'd found out she'd left suddenly, but she could hardly have done otherwise. That thought brought her full circle.

She pulled off a pair of dark glasses to rub tired eyes. The shades were a near permanent accessory now. She lay her head down on her desk, ready in that moment to weep. It was becoming too hard. Three times now she'd had to flee her office for an extended length of time. Three times she'd lied about it to coworkers and friends alike. One more time and she would likely be facing serious questions from her superiors about her ability to keep up her workload. Her father would be right, and she would fail. She was so tired.

Behind her eyelids she watched again the events of that horrible night replay like a tired movie. She couldn't escape the memory any more than she could escape the reality of her life since that moment. Once a month she changed, and became someone her father would not recognize. She became an animal.

Helen's intercom chose that moment to buzz sharply, pulling her back to the present. A second after she jerked upright, the door opened.

"I'm sorry, Helen…" Sherry Davis, Helen's receptionist, spoke quickly from the hall. "Mr. Sherman is here and insists on seeing you immediately." The middle-aged woman looked angrily over the top of her glasses at the man who pushed his way past her and through the door.

Helen stood to greet her uninvited guest. Her first impression of David Sherman tempted her to frown, although she held on to her pleasant expression as she'd trained herself to do. He was determined, and obviously irritated by her absence and her receptionist's protective attitude. Broad shouldered and thick through the chest, he towered over Sherry. Slightly too long, light brown hair flipped arrogantly over his brow, and a long nose and smooth, strong jaw finished the frame of his face. Only his hazel eyes stood out as exceptionally beautiful; they brought his features together into a very pleasing form.

Before Helen could quite associate this handsome man with the phone calls she'd received a week ago, he was in her office and having his own good look at her. She flushed slightly as his eyes roved, but she schooled her face into a pleasant mask. She was used to being inspected. It was all part of the business she had spent the last five years conquering.

She dressed the part of corporate executive-slash-warrior. Her tailored fuchsia suit fit her perfectly, and its bright color enhanced her pale skin and long black hair. She knew she looked tired, but as he stared at her longer and longer, she couldn't hold his gaze. What was he looking at? Could he see beyond her façade? Wondering brought an uneasy itch between her shoulder blades, but she refused to give in to the urge to hunch down in her chair.

"Ms. Mathews, I'm David Sherman. I'm glad to finally meet you." He extended his hand. His large, tanned fingers enclosed hers and she felt a tingle of attraction. She smiled at him, but sternly reminded herself of the many, many reasons

she could not possibly become involved with anyone
just now.

"Welcome, Mr. Sherman. I must apologize for not getting back to you sooner. I've been away on a business trip, as I'm sure my assistant informed you. I did, however, review the preliminary figures of your proposal."

Helen offered a chair with a wave of her hand as she lied though her teeth. She took her own seat, plunging into the details of the proposal. Without giving him an opportunity to comment on her absence, she lifted the page she thought indicated profit estimates, grateful that she'd at least had the time to pull the report from the pile of work on her desk and skim it before he arrived.

David reached for the paper, tugging it gently from her fingers. "Great percentages, don't you think? The lead indicators are well over the norm, and the market polls more than prove the need for these facilities in this location. It's hard to believe no one has acquired the land as yet." He smiled, looking pleased. His smile transformed his face from arrogant businessman to a ruggedly handsome man, and again she felt that zing of attraction.

"Yes, the numbers look interesting," Helen hedged. She had no idea what the percentages actually were, other than good.

"I'm glad to see you aren't letting a great deal slip away from Multoma. I was beginning to wonder if you were planning on passing it over to another firm." He looked at her calmly, apparently ignoring the fact that he was practically accusing her of stealing his pitch and perhaps even going behind the back of her own company. After a tense moment, his eyes shied to the left in a self-conscious movement.

"I see. Multoma does not operate that way, Mr. Sherman. Nor do I," she stated calmly. "My time is better spent as a negotiator than a thief." She kept her face composed, but her stomach clenched. So much for attraction. This was only the first of the problems and accusations she'd likely face by having a forced monthly absence from the company. At least the man before her had the grace to eventually look embarrassed by his suggestion. There were many who wouldn't care that they were being offensive, not when it came to business.

"Well, you can hardly blame me for my suspicions. Not after you seemed to disappear. Let me take you out to dinner tonight to make up for it." His attitude changed perceptibly. He was apparently going to accept her at her word. "We can discuss the proposal then, and you can have today to catch up on all the paperwork that built up while you were away."

He stood, and handed back the paper. "This page, by the way, doesn't have any percentage numbers on it." He smirked, just a bit, and lifted an eyebrow. The scent of his cologne—woodsy and male—reached her and the attraction returned, sharper now. "Perhaps you could read the report before tonight. I'll send you my car." He didn't wait for her answer, pressing the advantage of having caught her unprepared for his visit.

"That would be fine," she said as he walked out the door. "Just fine." She slumped back into her chair and held her head in her hands. "Shit. Cocky asshole. Sexy, cocky asshole."

2

David walked out of the office and into the elevator without losing his grin. He'd caught Helen Mathews at a disadvantage. Hard to say what her reason for being away really was, but it didn't seem to have anything to do with stealing his ideas, nor, he reflected, with business in general. That thought made him frown. Why had she endangered her career over the last three months? She was on the rise, but disappearing three times without a trace would put her accounts in jeopardy and make her a target for those who would want her position. He had to admit he hoped she hadn't run off to meet with some man. She presented a challenge—a powerful woman with a mystery, secrets that didn't seem as simple as an affair.

He hadn't expected her to be so sexy. He'd heard she was beautiful, but to be brutally honest, there weren't too many unattractive women who made it this far up the corporate ladder. In fact, not too many women made it this far at all, not that he agreed with the policy. But Helen Mathews was enough to make a man drool. She wasn't his normal type. He'd always preferred curvaceous little blondes. She was just about as opposite to his usual quarry as you could get: tall, with long, slender limbs and curves that were sweet, if trim. Her long black hair would look fantastic against his green satin pillowcases.

Now that was going too far. Provided she took up his business proposal, Helen Mathews would be a partner, if not his boss. She'd want control, of both the business and the personal side of things, he was sure. Just because she'd been caught off guard today, didn't mean she wasn't the steely-eyed witch he'd heard about.

Her eyes though…they were incredible. Had he ever seen eyes that color, so golden? They weren't contact lenses—he'd looked when he'd leaned over her desk to take the page of the report she hadn't read. They were huge and stunning, and they reflected warmth like it was a color of its own. They hid something though, and if they were going to be in business together, he'd have to find out what.

A bright red canopy capped the Ruby Foo's entrance. Although a good-sized line-up of people stood before the red and black lacquered doors waiting to get in, David ushered Helen past them and inside to the headwaiter's desk. They were motioned immediately to follow the Maitre D'. Helen had only a moment to take in the main dining area, but what she saw spiked her interest.

Red and gold colors dominated the room. Candles burning in black lacquered holders on each table accented the tablecloths and the Japanese symbols painted on them. Scarlet banners hung from the painted ceiling, and delicate watercolor and ink paintings graced every wall. The dark color of mahogany showed here and there on the leg of a table or chair.

She took a deep breath to absorb the enticing aromas that teased her senses. Hot and heady spices mingled with the cool scent of seafood. As they proceeded deeper into the restaurant, they passed a huge sushi bar. Two chefs stood before an open glass panel making seaweed rolls of fresh fish and rice. A constant hum of conversation, clinking utensils and subtle music rumbled in her ears. The room was packed with people—Ruby Foo's was a very trendy place to be. If David Sherman was trying to impress her with a private room here, he had achieved his goal.

She glanced around the room, movement drawing her attention in one direction after another. The noise began to ring in her ears. This was the first time in months she'd entered such a huge public place, and the atmosphere threatened to overwhelm her. She shifted closer to David, nearly stepping on the heels of the Maitre D'.

When they reached the end of the main dining room, the Maitre D' waved David and Helen in before him through a heavy looking, mahogany colored door. Inside was a tiny private dining room. The small room did not disappoint. It was decorated as generously in Japanese art as the main room, and the relief it provided Helen from the overpowering clashes of sensations of the larger space was more than welcome. She released a breath that she hadn't noticed she'd been holding. She smiled quickly as David caught her eye.

"I didn't know Ruby Foo's offered private dining rooms," she commented as she seated herself at the intimate table, the waiter hovering close by. "Since you base your operations out of Philadelphia, I'm surprised you know the place. They've only been open for a few months."

He simply raised an eyebrow at her. *Cocky man.*

As he pulled out his chair, she admired the cut of his dinner jacket and admitted to herself that she'd looked forward to the dinner, and the conversation. Since her problems began three months ago, she hadn't had a moment's relaxation.

The waiter attentively pushed in Helen's chair and laid a napkin across her lap. He handed them each a tall menu booklet, trimmed in the same red and gold of the décor.

"The menu is gigantic," she commented, simply to have something to say. "I can't decide what I want." As soon as she said that, she regretted it. After all, this was a business dinner, and she'd just shown a form of weakness to the man opposite her, even if it was a tiny indecision.

David looked up from his own menu and smiled knowingly. "I'm for some *negitoro temaki sushi* to start, and then I want the ginger shrimp with peppers and Savoy cabbage. It's wonderful." His smile deepened. "Want some suggestions? Or are you familiar with Japanese food?"

"I'm fine, thanks. I think the chef's choice *dim sum* appetizers and the *tempura* crab are for me." She regained her composure, and took charge. "So you've been here before."

"Yes, a couple of months ago, when I was here checking up on your firm." He smiled, taking the sting out of the reminder of his accusations that afternoon. "Everything here is good."

"Were you alone?" she asked, and then flushed, knowing how that comment must have sounded. Why did she want to know, anyway?

David hesitated then spoke, his voice a low, sexy drawl. "That's a mighty personal question, Ms. Mathews. Are we talking business or pleasure tonight?" His eyes slid to her mouth, and she fought a shiver.

"Business, of course." Helen straightened her shoulders, glad she'd decided against a more revealing change of clothes for the evening. A business suit was a shield, of sorts. She reached for her briefcase and pulled out a sheaf of papers. As she laid them on the table, she thought she saw a flash of disappointment cross her companion's face. She didn't comment on it. It would be best if she could keep this meeting as professional as possible, relaxation be damned. The waiter chose that moment to arrive to take their drink orders, breaking the tension.

After she ordered a glass of white wine, and David ordered a bottle of hot *sake*, Helen cleared the centerpiece from the table and spread out several reports. "I think, with what you have proposed, this office center could be very successful. However, Multoma has a somewhat different agenda than the retail areas you have in mind. We've had some great successes combining community planning with office planning or retail development."

"What I see, when I look at your concept, is a gap. You have office spaces and retail spaces, but similar developments are already located and underused nearby. What I think would create a better draw to the office environment is a professional center, a location to draw in a series of doctor's offices, perhaps legal facilities and, if we're lucky, a spa." She paused, and looked up from the papers to find David staring intently at her.

"Is there a problem, Mr. Sherman?" Helen considered his expression and wondered if he was going to reject the idea of Multoma putting its own stamp on the project. If that were the case, he could look elsewhere for a developer, and it wasn't too likely that he'd find one that would accept his proposal without making a few changes.

David took a mouthful of sake, his expression vague, as he savored the rice wine for longer than necessary.

"No," he said, and poured another tiny glassful for himself and a second, which he pushed in front of Helen. "I'm considering the motive behind this suggestion. It wouldn't have to do with the fact that Multoma owns a good chunk of that nearby, underused retail space, would it?" He raised his eyes to Helen's.

A second waiter arrived to take their meal order and Helen breathed an inaudible sigh of relief. Of course Multoma owned those shops, and her directive was to ensure that any new development would bring more public traffic into the area. More retail space would do that, but wouldn't necessarily increase the rental value of their properties. David surely knew that. He was simply baiting her, trying to imply that Multoma was only interested in his project as a means to improve their own holdings.

"Of course it does. It also has to do with the fact that the government is planning on building its first seniors' center in the area, one planned to be a nearly self-sufficient town. These facilities will go hand in hand with the government's project, increase foot and local traffic, and everyone will benefit." Helen gave him a straight look, daring him to continue to taunt her. She ignored the drink he'd poured for her. This was a good project, but not the only fish in the sea.

"Okay, so we agree on the development of the area, and the office complex, and I am willing to review your plans on the professional center. Is your company officially interested?" David waited.

"If it weren't, I wouldn't be here. Do we have a deal then?"

"A probationary one at least, while we work out the details." David held out his hand to shake on the deal and seal it. Helen clasped her hand in his and for a moment, neither said a word, and neither let go.

His skin was warm, his hand large on hers. Attraction sizzled up her arm and down her spine. It was a challenge, the way he was staring, daring her to be the first to break eye contact or let go. She let a small smile play over her lips, trying to show him she recognized his intent without having to comment on it. After all, she knew all about alpha male attitudes. The first one to look away would be admitting they were the weaker of the two. Since she never could give up a challenge, this would make for an interesting partnership, as they felt each other out and looked for any weakness. And, if nothing else, this moment allowed her to appreciate his gorgeous eyes.

The early arrival of the waiter carrying their appetizers drew the contest to an end, with Helen and David exchanging a sardonic smile as they both let go. A simple staring match would never settle dominance in their partnership, and they both knew it, but it was difficult to resist. They quickly set aside the proposal papers and Helen turned her attention to the steaming dish of dim sum before her. Steam rose from the ceramic bowl of dumplings; the delicate aroma of fish and spices made her mouth water. She almost wiggled in anticipation of the subtle flavors that were sure to match those scents.

It was then that she noticed an equally interesting aroma coming from David's plate. As she focused her attention on his plate of sushi, the wild scent of raw fish and pressed seaweed became overpowering. She couldn't prevent her tongue from slipping between her teeth to lick her lips. David made an odd noise and she glanced up at him. The masculine odor of his skin mixed seductively with his cologne. She breathed him in, absorbed his particular scent, stronger now than it had been in the office. It was heady stuff, and she smiled at the one newfound ability her curse provided her that she actually enjoyed—a stronger sense of smell.

David leaned toward her over the dinner table. "Don't stop. I love it when a beautiful woman looks at me like she might devour me." His voice was husky, and drew her eyes to his lips. They were full and sensual, and she thought she might like to bite them. He tapped her lips with a pair of chopsticks, breaking her flash of desire.

"Sorry. Your dinner looks wonderful, and I was wondering if perhaps I should have ordered sushi as well," Helen hedged. *What was she thinking? Yes, he's handsome, and powerful, and intelligent. He's also a business prospect, and a known womanizer. Get a grip!*

"Try some." He offered a roll carefully with his chopsticks, and she had little choice but to accept it from him. He fed her carefully, dragging the chopsticks over her lips and watching her as she chewed the delicate morsel slowly. Without a doubt he was teasing her. She couldn't resist it—she licked her lips again, this time giving him a provocative glance beneath lowered eyelids. Her own appetizer lay cooling in front of her, but she ignored it, preferring to prolong the mocking sensuality that bounced between them. Some things, even things she knew couldn't go anywhere, were meant to be enjoyed.

They returned to their separate meals, eating in a not-quite-comfortable silence. It was too electric to be comfortable. She stole glances at him, while he stared at her lips. Did he want a kiss? Helen wanted one…and yet, she didn't. Teasing was one thing, but a kiss would take them over the edge of what was allowed professionally. And after all the craziness of the last three months, well, she wasn't sure what would happen if she tried to take things to a physical level.

David leaned closer, looking at her eyes, and Helen looked away. She could only imagine what he thought of her odd eye coloring. Perhaps he thought she wore special contact lenses to appear more exotic. The color certainly wasn't natural, but it was one of those things she was slowly becoming accustomed to. Time to cut dinner short.

"Thank you for introducing me to Ruby Foo's. It's been interesting. My office will be in contact with yours on

Monday to send you our revised proposal." She opted for her most businesslike tone and stood up from the table, and it seemed effective in backing him off a little. If anything were going to happen between them, *she* would be the one in control, not him.

David stood as well and grinned. "But I'll see you tomorrow. I've got one more day in New York, and I expect you to spend a little of it with me, as my new partner…and all."

Helen pursed her lips in frustration. How could she say no? He was laughing at her, but she had to comply. "Fine. Why don't we meet for lunch?"

"Sounds good. After we take a look at the site, of course. I like to get my bearings physically before I make any final decisions about building. I've been there before, but I'd like to see it through your eyes. I'll pick you up at ten o'clock." He swept his fingers through his hair, his voice charmingly smooth.

"No, I'll meet you at the site. I'd rather take my SUV."

"Ooh, a woman who enjoys the feeling of power under her. My mom always said to look out for women who drove big trucks," he teased.

She shook her head, having trouble associating the laughing man with the serious businessman, the same way she'd thought it difficult to associate the demanding and accusing agent with the sexy man before her.

"Right then," he said, stepping away from the table. "I'll meet you at my site in the morning."

He was pressing her again, pushing her to follow his lead. His site. For now, she ignored it, but tomorrow would be different. She'd show him it would be her plans, not his, that directed the development. Having another successful project under her name would shut everyone up, absences or no.

3

It was only six o'clock in the morning. Helen stared at her wardrobe and sighed. How did she pick out clothes that said 'Yes, I'm tough, and good at what I do, but I'm also a woman outside the office, not that I care if you notice'? That was a complicated message and said something about her interest in David that she could little afford. On the practical side, it would also have to be something she could stomp around the potential development site in, and that might be a little rough.

At last she decided on a semi-casual ensemble that consisted of a single-breasted linen blazer and silk shell top, and contrasting blue jeans and leather ankle boots. The blazer and shell were a pale, frosted-blue, and looked great with her black hair. Even better, the jeans made her long legs a focal point, without resorting to another skirt. The whole selection process had destroyed her closet. When was the last time she'd taken this much time with her appearance? The answer came quickly. The last time was the night of the annual company party, and that was something she didn't want to think about just now.

She dressed quickly, efficiently. A quick trip to the mirror and a few flicks of her brush tamed her wild hair. Make-up was minimal. She certainly wasn't going to try to encourage the man. She had a feeling he'd be doing that all on his own, despite his words about business first.

Her own inclinations were going to be firmly squashed, at least when it came to David. She reached absently for her favorite silver bracelet, thinking about his broad shoulders. A sudden burst of pain shot through her hand and she screamed in both frustration and agony as she threw the offending piece of jewelry across the room.

Helen fisted her burning hand, fingers wrapped tightly against the pain there. She squeezed her eyes tight as she stood in front of the mirror. Those damn yellow eyes! A sob escaped her lips. It didn't matter what she wore, or what she looked like, now. Of course business would come first. It would come last, too. There was no way she was ever going to have a personal relationship again, not in this condition. She opened her eyes. The golden color was still there. She opened her hand. Although the pain was gone, a blistered patch of red glared up at her from her palm.

Chill air crept down the back of David's neck. He glanced around quickly. Where the hell was he? An intense growling sounded close by and his heart raced. He was in the woods, but where? How? The trees around him cast deep black shadows, although the moon glowed above—a full round circle of silver light.

The tree limbs stood bare of leaves; layers of snow trimmed each branch and the ground around him. The low-pitched, rumbling growl reached him again, and the sensation of being watched competed with the cold air to send shivers down his back.

Slowly, he turned in a circle, scanning the darkness between the pools of moonlight. Something moved. He caught another flicker off to his left. There was more than one of the creatures in the woods, watching him. The beating of his heart seemed louder now than the crunch of the snow at his feet. The only other noises were the harsh gasps he made as he tried to get enough air, and the soft growls he continued to hear from the trees. Four sets of golden eyes shone out at him from the shadows.

A crashing noise reverberated through the clearing where David stood. He whirled toward the racket, shocked by the sound. A flash of white preceded his realization that what he was seeing was a woman. She fled like a wounded deer through the forest, breaking small branches as she went and crying out in pain and fear. She rushed toward him, and he grasped then that the white color was her naked flesh.

The woman raced closer, her dark hair streaming out behind her. Her body was fantastic. She had long supple limbs, shapely breasts and a narrow waist that drew his eyes down toward her feminine core. Then he realized her hands and feet were coated in mud. Welts covered her legs and arms. She looked at him through her pain, and cried soundlessly for help. It was Helen Mathews.

Her eyes reflected the same golden color as those from the darkness in the woods. David whipped around, checking for the creatures that had been watching him. There was no sign of anything, but howls called from where Helen had breached the woods, sounding a call for the hunt.

She reached him and grabbed at his hands. "Run!" She panted the words out. "Run for your life!" She dragged him with her, and then stumbled. David looked back as he heard the howling start again. Great gray wolves stalked them, growing closer, grinning in their toothy way at prey that could not escape. He turned to Helen. She was grinning now too, her eyes golden in the moonlight. He dropped her hand, and she began to howl. He ran, ran and...

David woke, gasping for breath. He clutched at the bedding, sweat drenching his body and dampening the soft cotton sheets. He sat up, and nearly died on the spot as he took in the wolf across from his bed in the early morning light. Then he slumped to the mattress as he recognized it as the poster he'd purchased from the National Conservation Organization.

"Holy crap. Wolves and naked women equal too much business and not enough sex." Still, his heart pounded and he could remember the vision of Helen, beautiful, naked, and in pain.

It had to be their sexually charged meeting last night and the anticipation of their meeting this morning that caused the dream. Mix that liberally with the mystery of her unexplained absence and a dose of the wildlife channel before bed last night and bang—one hair-raising subconscious experience. The problem with that little theory though, was that it was obvious that she was on his mind, and under his skin. That hadn't happened in a long time. Not since Sharon. And Sharon was dead.

He rolled out of bed, the soft sheets falling away from his naked body. A slight chill ran down his spine as cool air touched drying sweat. A shower first, then coffee, and then he'd tackle his approach to Ms. Mathews. If he could get her to admit what she'd been doing last week some of the mystery would disappear. As less of an enigma, she would be less of a challenge and less of an interest, at least on a personal level. He hoped. While a challenge was good, he didn't need a woman who would want to take over and rule his life.

***

Most of the proposed site was swamp. Not the sort that wildlife experts would call home to any important species though; this mess was caused by humans alone and was new and raw, no doubt caused by the construction somewhere further up the river, probably last year's series of new strip-malls.

Helen scanned the brush and caught movement here and there, but found little of interest. Windborne trash, mostly. She kept her breathing shallow. There was a scent of dead *something* nearby, and although some small part of her insisted she investigate, sniff it out, she kept her feet firmly planted on dry ground. She wouldn't let the change direct her if she could stop it.

She couldn't help her reaction, though, when her ears caught the sound of an approaching vehicle. Her body swiveled toward the sound and her stance altered to a more challenging posture. She resisted the urge to open her mouth to taste the air, but inhaled deeply as a man stepped from the now-parked Jeep. David. His scent carried to her on the breeze and her posture changed again as a tingle of pleasure slid through her body, causing her breasts to peak with inter-est. *Damn.*

He was dressed as casually as she. His jeans were molded to his legs—tight around thick thighs and narrow hips. An open, lightweight navy jacket rippled with the breeze, doing little to stop the air from lifting it away from his torso. Under the jacket he wore a collared Polo-style shirt, unbut-toned, in royal blue. At the open neck a tiny swatch of thick dark body hair peeked through, hinting at a larger, rougher patch below. Helen licked suddenly dry lips.

"Hey," he called out to her, still some distance away.

She waved and turned back to look again at the site, noting the highway in the background that would provide access. The seniors' village would be to the left, giving some of the new residents a nice view of the river.

Pretending indifference to David's approach was difficult when she could hear his sneakers against the dead grass and dirt groundcover. The swish of his cotton jeans rubbing together at his upper thighs. Her body hummed as it raced to interpret the signals of the approaching male. *If I concentrated, could I hear his heartbeat? Better not try.*

"Well, you beat me here. What do you think?" David's voice carried to her as he paced the last few steps to reach her side.

"I think it's going to work. Better than that, it's going to work well, both for the people who use the facilities, and for Multoma. Since you already own part of the land, it's going to work well for you too." She turned to look at him and saw the excitement in his eyes. "This is your biggest development yet, isn't it?"

"Yup." He grinned. "Not as big as your last creation, but I'm proud of it."

She felt her lips thin and tried to prevent a frown from appearing on her face. Her last big project had had a few too many complications. Certainly one that was beyond unexpected; it was ruining her life.

"Have you made sure there are no claims to the land? Even from people who don't own it, but perhaps just use it? Have you checked the history of the land?" she pressed. "No animal rights people, no Native Americans who hold meetings here, no summer fairs or anything?"

He cocked his head to one side, obviously puzzled. The question of who might use the land other than owners wasn't usually addressed, particularly this sort of vacant land to the side of the city proper.

"Why? Have you heard something? Is there going to be a problem because it's a wetland? It hasn't been a swamp for long; I don't think we'll see any conservationists here. It's just scrub. That's what makes it so perfect for the project." He rubbed one had over his jaw line.

"I want a complete report on usage before Multoma

offers any contract. I had some problems with the Detroit plan that I don't want repeated." She crossed her arms.

He stared at her, his eyes seeming to try to penetrate the protection of her dark glasses.

"What problem did you have exactly? I never heard about anything."

She licked her lips. How much could she say? "We had a group of itinerates who used a small parcel of the land complain that we'd broached their rights as squatters. They claimed a history of use of the land as a group, much like a Native American claim to sacred land."

"Obviously it didn't hold up in court. How did you keep it so quiet?"

"It never made it to court. The group chose not to take it to the papers, and we sure weren't about to. So, I want this land checked. I don't want any more groups mad at me, or rather at Multoma. I don't want anyone out there ready to throw curses or try to ruin our reputation." She turned from him, her shoulders stiffening under what she was sure was the pressure of his eyes on her back. That shouldn't have slipped out that way. Now he was going to be curious.

Curses? What the hell was that supposed to mean? David stared at her rigid body. He was used to dealing with some unusual requests for assurances on development deals, particularly when any legal entanglements might be involved, but her reaction was a bit extreme. Just what had happened in Detroit?

He watched her for a moment more, but she didn't move. She seemed to be waiting for him to say something. His eyes lingered on her long black hair. Draped in a braid down her back, it pointed like an arrow to the soft curves of her buttocks visible under the edge of her jacket.

Finally it came to him, a small detail. He'd heard a bit of a water cooler joke about the woman in front of him. At the last Multoma bash, Helen Mathews had not only been cheered as a shark by her own president, she'd been screamed at by some old woman who had crashed through security. Some party.

"That crazy woman at your party…" he began.

She whipped around, her face aflame. "So you heard about that?" She leaned forward aggressively, unfolding her arms and fisting her hands. Her jaw thrust toward him. Her face, from under the dark shades, wore a grimace of anger. "Heard about the Gypsy curse? Heard I was shaking in my boots after some nut called me names? Well, that has nothing to do with this. Nothing to do with the way I do business. I just don't want to have any more possible legal problems pop up unexpectedly on one of my projects."

"Whoa, hold it." He raised his hands between them. "I didn't hear anything, just that there had been some nut at the party. Was she part of the group that threatened the Detroit deal?"

"They didn't threaten anything. The deal went through just fine. The Rom wanted to keep their meeting space, but it was put to a better use. That hospital serves thousands. I got the job done."

He reached out to touch her, to break the mood. She stepped back before his hand could reach her linen jacket.

"Let's go. The site will be fine. As soon as you bring the usage report, we'll amend the contract as we discussed last night and present it to you. After you approve, we'll send it to the inspectors and have an environmental report run. We don't need to be here any longer. Besides, that dead rat is really beginning to stink."

She stalked off, her back ramrod straight. David blinked after her. She was a bundle of nerves. What the hell had that been all about? Gypsies? He looked around and took a deep breath. The air was fresh and cool, the late spring air untainted. What dead rat? He needed Multoma, but did he need a crazy woman for a partner?

He paced after her, reaching his Jeep moments after she slammed the door shut on her SUV. They were supposed to go for lunch after visiting the site, but really hadn't discussed where. If he didn't say something to her right now, he knew she'd take it as an excuse to bow out of any further time alone with him. If they were going to work together he had to know whatever the hell was going on with her wouldn't affect the job. He turned back to her vehicle and walked to the driver's door. As he approached he caught her image in the side view mirror. She had her shades off and was rubbing her eyes.

There was nothing worse than a woman with tears in her eyes.

A quick knock on the window brought those odd golden eyes up to meet his. They were molten gold, the hot color of liquid metal. Hot enough to heat his blood even through the glass. She rolled the window down and raised her eyebrows.

"How about we go to an early lunch at the Apple Barrel? I love their pie." He tried for his most charming smile and watched her gloomy expression become even grimmer.

"I'm not getting personally involved with you, Mr. Sherman. Last night I may have given you the wrong impression. I don't mix business with pleasure. And it's too early for lunch."

Her rejection was strong and dismissive, her voice cold. If it weren't for the misery in her eyes and the understanding that she was hiding something, something to do with her earlier reaction to his mention of the crazy woman at the

Multoma party, he would have stopped right there. Instead, his interest was piqued further. So much for removing the air of mystery about her this morning and getting back to business. Ms. Matthews was simply more challenging than he had thought.

"I have another development I'm considering, a mountain resort. I'd like to discuss some prelims with you, as a separate arrangement with Multoma. We could do that over pie. And we'll call it brunch, not lunch." He smiled again, although part of him seriously objected about sharing information on another project when they hadn't even signed the contract for the first one.

Her mouth worked and she bit her lip. Was the decision really so hard? She must really have something to hide from him. But she looked so close to the edge… He tried again. "It's a spa-slash-retreat. Something really decadent. Something just for pleasure."

"Something I'm sure you know all about," she murmured. She bit her lip again, an unconscious gesture that heated him to the bone, the flash of her sharp white teeth against her blood red lips.

"Business *is* pleasure. Do you really want to give up the satisfaction we could bring each other?"

4

She was definitely a weak woman. Brunch together was such a bad idea. But she let herself be convinced on the pretext of the business to come today. Really, it was for the chance to feel normal for a few minutes. He didn't know everything about her. Not that her few friends or associates had more than a clue or two as to the problem she faced, but he hadn't met her before the change and wouldn't be able to see how different she'd become.

For one thing, she ate a lot more. Brunch was such an easy meal to tuck into: bacon and pancakes and muffins, sausages, croissants, and omelets. She tried to make it less obvious and loaded the plate with protein which called to her more anyway, but he didn't seem to notice. He ate his own meal with gusto, unconcerned as men always seemed to be about eating in public. And he was going to eat apple pie after this? He had to be joking.

She took a sip of coffee and nearly spit it out. When had coffee become so disgusting? Just another change that the Rom had cursed her with. She clenched her fists under the table and put her cup down quickly before she cracked it.

"Problem?" David had put down his fork after cleaning his plate. How long had he been finished? Had he seen her reaction to coffee? Did she have to worry about every change in her expression and every single thing she did from now on?

Maybe coming here had been a worse mistake than she'd thought.

"No, just bad coffee. I'm thinking of giving it up anyway."

He picked up his coffee cup and took a sip. "Tastes good to me."

He seemed to be watching her pretty carefully. Who could blame him? Who would want to go into business with someone like her now? He probably thought she was crazy, the way she was acting.

"Let's talk about the mountain resort." He leaned back in his chair, clearly relaxed when she was anything but. What was his game?

"Okay, tell me what you have in mind."

She listened while he talked. He was definitely smart enough to create a plan that would make them a lot of money. Just like the one they were about to embark on together. If she made it that far. How long could she keep up the charade? She was already feeling the pressure of her absences from work and the change was growing worse.

The change. How else could she think of it but as *the change*? There was her life before the Rom, and her life after. Her changed life.

Every month it got worse. First her eyes, then her reaction to silver, the heightened senses, and now her impossible-to-fight attraction to a man who was basically a stranger. What would happen next? And of course none of this compared to what caused her monthly absences from work. That change was something she wouldn't bring herself to think about.

David pulled out a set of documents from his briefcase. The papers detailing his ideas on the mountain resort were very preliminary. It was something much more like a retreat, far from everything and high on a mountain that his family had owned a large portion of for generations. On the very far edge of the state, the low mountain seemed like a haven. A place far from the world. She'd have to start thinking about how far away she'd need to go this month. Where she could go. Her last hideaway was unavailable now, preparing for the summer season and filled with care-takers. Soon there would be campers both young and old; the Lakeside Campground was the last place she could hide.

"Is there a direct road to the proposed development?"

David seemed surprised at her interjection. "Yes, but not much of one. There's an old logging road that we sometimes use. Last time I was up there was with some surveyors to review the borders. That was eight months ago."

"So your family doesn't use this property at all anymore?"

"No, although there is an old hunting cabin my dad used to use. He passed away a few years ago."

"I'm sorry. It's pretty far from any major city or airport." She considered the ramifications of that. Possibly good for her, probably bad for any development.

"That's the point. It's pristine. People will go so they can experience wildlife and a natural setting but with every comfort a spa can provide." He grinned.

"Wildlife? What kind of wildlife?" She toyed with her fork. Maybe that was too far away, two wild.

"The usual—deer, rabbits, coyotes, bears, maybe wolves." He was looking at her strangely. It wasn't that unusual question, who wouldn't be concerned or interested with the wildlife? The idea of deer and rabbits sounded interesting…

"Helen… Your eyes…"

She clenched the fork in her hand hard and stared at him. What was wrong with her eyes now?

"Your eyes are glowing."

She dropped the fork stood and gathered her purse. "Yes, the sun is right in my eyes. And I really need to get going. It's been lovely, thank you. When you have a more formal report I'd like to hear about this resort again. And of course I'll be waiting for the usage report on the initial development. Perhaps we can meet next week."

***

She was gone again and this time he didn't stop her. Maybe that was a good thing. What had he just seen? A trick of the light? He gathered his papers from the table. She seemed interested in his new idea. Hell, who wouldn't be? It was a good one. Taking her to brunch had been a good idea, hadn't it? She'd certainly been hungry, putting away a huge plate of the brunch buffet. He enjoyed a woman who ate when they were hungry, rather than picking away at some salad because they thought they had to look concerned with their weight at all times. But then, her eyes... No way that was the sun in her eyes, was it? They were beside the window, but...

He picked up the last paper and glanced at her place setting. Slowly, he reached over and picked up her fork. He sat back in his chair stared at the utensil. After a moment he glanced around and carefully put it in his pocket. Unlike the other utensils at their table, it was noticeably twisted and now bore the distinct imprints of fingers.

***

Would this day never end? Helen signed off on yet another report. The pile had been steadily growing for the last nine hours she'd been in the office. Catching up was going to kill her. The words were blurring together, although she felt good about her progress. Maybe it was simply time to quit and go home.

But what was waiting for her there? Nothing. How had she never noticed how empty her apartment felt? She had no family and only the memories of her father driving her to succeed at work. What did that even matter now? Why had she thought beating his expectations mattered years after he died? Her problems were a hell of a lot worse than that now. Once, her father had pushed her because she wasn't the son he'd wanted. He'd never been satisfied. But because her mother had died when she was only a child, he'd been all she had. And pleasing him had become more than a challenge, it had become an obsession.

Now her problems were somewhere in the vicinity of the moon, if you put the difference between expectations from an overbearing parent on one end of a scale and measured the distance to her current issue: her body changing with the coming of the moon. She wasn't even human anymore, so what did it matter that she wasn't a man, wasn't a son to a man who was dead and gone?

She signed off on her computer and stretched in her chair. There were no friends to worry about either, not really. She had no time for friends and work associates didn't count. What could they bring her when her only goal was to climb the corporate ladder higher and higher? She stood and walked to the door and slapped the light off as she crossed the threshold. The office was deserted. She had sent Sherry and Taryn home long ago. Sherry had a family and Taryn… well, the woman had more boyfriends than you could count. It was probably date night.

It was something Helen could almost envy. Almost, because the men never seemed to stay very long. Taryn's choice, apparently. Helen would prefer something, someone, who stuck around. Someone she could count on. She walked to the elevator and pressed the button. There were a few lights on in some of the junior offices. Keeners working hard to get ahead, just like she had. Her last boyfriend, if she could call him that, had been just like them—just like her. She couldn't say when she'd spoken to him last. Apparently it hadn't mattered that much to either of them.

Good God, she was pathetic. Thinking about all this when she only had two weeks left before she'd have to run again. What would a boyfriend matter then? No one could help her. When she had first understood what the Rom had done to her, she'd been furious. She still was. She didn't deserve it. All she'd done was her job.

They had made her into something out of a horror story. Some days, it seemed like she'd lost her mind, that stress had taken its toll and she'd gone off the deep end. Had she ever in her life believed that magic was real? That the moon could change her reality into something completely other? That she'd look at the glowing ball hanging in the night sky and howl…and like it?

The elevator took her to the parking level and she waved to the attendant before she walked to her SUV. She'd always preferred to drive herself, even after she could afford a driver. One man had called her a control freak and maybe that was true. But now driving was one of the few things she could still control in her life.

In minutes she was at her apartment parking lot. She parked in her spot and shut off the engine but couldn't bring herself to get out. Her arms and legs weighed tons and her head ached. A hot bath sounded perfect but getting out of the SUV and going up to the apartment seemed like a lot of effort.

"This is not good. You're getting weaker, Helen. Isn't that

what Dad would say? You're weak?" As always, the voice of her father drove her into action. She would get through this. She had two weeks. And a plan. She got out of the vehicle and made her way to the lobby. No way was she letting go of everything she'd achieved. She'd get caught up at work and then she'd use the excuse of checking out the mountain David owned for possible development to get away. That would take care of this month's change.

Her step faltered. And next month? She lifted her head and strode on toward the elevator. Before next month, she'd find those damn Gypsies. She had to.

"Package for you, Miss Mathews," the apartment doorman called out to her.

Helen detoured to the main desk and forced a smile. "Thanks, Ed. I wasn't expecting anything."

The doorman shrugged and offered her package about a foot square in size, wrapped in brown paper and covered in stamps. She took it, thanked him, and headed for the elevator again. The box was light but then everything seemed to be these days. She couldn't quite get used to the change in her strength, although it was nice to be able to handle things with ease that she might have struggled with a few months ago.

She fished the keys from her purse and walked from the elevator to her apartment, one of the two penthouses. She put the box on the side table and headed straight for the bar. Wine didn't do much for her anymore but she still enjoyed the taste, maybe more so now. Every flavor was enhanced and she enjoyed the minor notes of the wine as well as any connoisseur. If land development didn't work out, she could go into business as a taster. She poured a glass of red and chuckled at the thought. What would her father think if she spent every day tasting luscious wines owned by rich men and women?

He'd be furious, that's for sure. He'd say that she was wasting her life. She lost her amusement. Work was always more important than enjoyment; power preferable to pleasure.

She looked around her apartment. Everything was perfect. And empty. She'd fallen right in with his plans for her, always wanting to please him. And now he was gone, she'd kept going, his voice still in her mind, still pushing. She really didn't know anything else.

On Monday, it was like the dam had broken in the office. She stood in front of the espresso machine in the coffee room and listened to the buzz. Everyone had waited for her to reveal what she had been doing over the last few months, jetting away from work without a word to anyone. Now the waiting had stopped and since she hadn't been forthcoming, the questions had begun. She had her excuses ready; her cover story about investigating David Sherman's propositions from different vantage points prepared in detail. Some people accepted it and moved on. After all, everyone knew she was work centric.

Sherry and Taryn clearly didn't buy her story. The looks they gave her were doubtful at best. But they didn't push and for that she was grateful. On the other hand, she wasn't totally prepared after all, when her boss arrived at her office door and leaned against the frame, sporting the same skeptical look.

"Look, Helen, I think you know what I'm here to say. If you're getting ready to move on, if you're researching other firms or deals that won't involve Multoma, I need you to be clear about it up front. Word is getting around and it doesn't look good for us or you."

Helen stood. "Mr. Winfield, I'm not planning on moving

on. I like my position here very much. I've simply been investigating —"

"Don't give me that, Helen. Sherman's proposals don't require trips out of state. Yes, I know you left the state. I know a lot about what goes on around here." He straightened up and stepped inside her office. "If it's something else, if you need someone to talk to… Things haven't been right since the award night. Is it about the hospital deal? Did something happen that wasn't legal? The way that woman pursued us legally and then just let things go…"

"No." Helen came around her desk, her heart pounding. "No. Everything I did was perfectly legal. We bought the rights to that land and we gave it a use that will help all the people in the city. The Gypsies dropped the case because they didn't have a leg to stand on."

"Gypsies—so the lawyer who caused all the fuss *was* part of that group. That old woman, she was the lawyer."

Winfield was too sharp. His mind was clicking along making connections she couldn't afford him to think on too long. Her claims aside, he'd soon be sure she was doing something the company wouldn't want to be involved with. She would *not* lose this job. She'd fought too hard to get it. She ground her teeth together.

Winfield took a step back. He was staring at her. Goddammit! Was it her eyes again? This was so not good. She turned away. "Look, Mr. Winfield, I've worked hard for this company, hard for you. I'm not about to jeopardize what I've achieved here—what we've achieved here. I've got some things going on but it'll all be sorted out soon." It had to be.

"Maybe you should take some time off. Get things sorted out sooner rather than later."

She turned back to him. "Maybe I should. I've got some work to do but then I'll take my leave for a few weeks. I'll get the Sherman deal closed first."

Winfield took another step back. He was already past the threshold. "Take all the time you need." He quietly shut the door.

She stood there and stared at the enameled wood panel for several minutes. If she didn't stop the change from happening soon, she could kiss her life goodbye.

5

What the hell was he doing, sitting outside her apartment like a stalker? People got arrested for crap like this. He had to be out of his mind. He fingered the fork in his jacket pocket, the one he brought with him everywhere the one Helen had warped and twisted with the simple clenching of her fist. Nope, he wasn't crazy. At least not for thinking they were something really wrong going on. For getting involved? For that, he might be crazy. He should just move on work with another developer, but Multoma was the best and he couldn't quite bring himself to request a different representative—that would ruin her career. And what if he was wrong?

He spotted her car pulling in. He waited a couple of minutes then got out of his car and walked into the lobby. The doorman looked at him, clearly about to question his appearance when Helen stepped out of the parking elevator. "Helen," he called to her. "I've been waiting for you." He walked closer. He had to keep this normal, friendly, or she'd have the doorman call the cops.

Her eyebrows lifted as she recognized him, but she kept

her poise. "What are you doing here, Mr. Sherman? This is quite inappropriate."

He took her by the elbow and whispered, "We need to talk." She tried to shake him off but he held on. "I don't think you really want to make a scene, do you?"

She glared at him but it was definitely time to find out what was going on. Finally she nodded and waved off the doorman. David followed her into the second elevator that ran to the apartments. As soon as the doors closed she yanked her elbow from his grip.

"I don't know what you think you're doing, but I will not be manhandled."

He stepped up close to her, getting in her face. "I want to know what's going on. And you're going to tell me."

She snarled and gave him a shove, dead in the center of his chest. He stumbled backward. She was a lot stronger than she looked, but then, he knew that. He hadn't expected her to be so aggressive. His heart leaped in his chest and he smiled. It was damned exciting. She looked amazing, just a little bit angry and seriously sexy.

"You don't really want to know." Her chest heaved, and her lips trembled.

"I've got to know. My business is my life and I can't get involved with your company without knowing what the hell is going on with you." He took a step closer.

"You wouldn't believe me." Her voice held the slightest quaver. She was on the edge of telling him; he could see it in her eyes—those beautiful golden eyes.

The elevator came to a stop and the doors opened. She glanced at the doors but didn't move. He reached out and touched her shoulder gently. "You can trust me." Maybe it was the whole thing about seeing a woman in trouble, but whatever she had to say he was going to listen and he was going to help her.

Mutely, Helen walked out of the elevator and approached one of the apartment doors. It was a short corridor with only four apartment doorways. Hers was the first on the left. She frowned at the obviously new addition—a handprint scanner as part of a security system—and his pulse quickened. She'd added security recently, and wasn't happy about it. She laid her palm on the scanner and when it beeped admission, pulled out a key and unlocked the door. Inside, there was a chain lock and two bolts, one high up on the door. Far more security than you would need in this part of town.

Not a good sign.

She walked to a small bar, laid her purse down, and dropped her briefcase. Her hands shook slightly as she poured two fingers of brandy into an uncut glass. She took a long drink.

"Mind if I have a drink?" She seemed to have forgotten he was there and startled at his voice.

She pulled back her shoulders, straightening. Maybe she was going to change her mind about talking to him. But she poured him a drink and handed it to him before pouring herself another.

"Have a seat." She gestured to the small seating area near the windows overlooking the city. She walked to the chair nearest the window and dropped onto the cushion.

"I don't know what you want me to tell you or what you think is happening. Yes, I've been out of town recently. I've been to see family and I've been away checking on different projects. And none of it is your business."

So, she was going to try to put him off again. He took a sip of the brandy. It was the good stuff, rich with deep tones. It heated his throat while he thought about what to say next. How he handled the next few minutes could make or break their partnership and would either get him the truth or get him thrown out.

"I can't begin a partnership with lies, Helen. And you are lying. We both know it. Your secretary's been covering for you, but she doesn't know where you've been." He toyed with his glass. Maybe another angle here. "She cares about you. So does your receptionist and both of them are worried."

She frowned but he cut her off before she could say anything. "No, they didn't tell me. Your staff is loyal. But I read people very well. I can tell when they're lying, just like I can tell you're lying. So what are you hiding?"

"I… I'm thinking of leaving the company." She shifted slightly in the chair and crossed her legs. Damn, she had hot legs.

"Also a lie."

The corners of her mouth tipped down slightly. She'd lost most of her lipstick and her eyes looked tired, but she'd lost none of her appeal. He pulled the fork from his pocket. He toyed with it with one hand, and watched her while he took a sip of brandy. He didn't miss the way her eyes widened at the appearance of the twisted utensil. She jumped to her feet and paced back to the bar where she tossed back her drink.

"I think you should go. If you don't want to work with me, that's fine. I'll assign another developer, unless you want to give up on Multoma." She turned back to him. Her mouth held a grimace. "They are the best, though. You aren't likely to get a better deal or have a better person manage it."

He stood and walked to her, leaned closer while he set the glass on the counter. "I know." He took her glass from her and she let him, though he could see the tension in her jaw. He set her glass beside his. "You *are* the best. And I want you." He meant it in so many ways and tried to tell her a few of them with his tone.

She closed her eyes for a second, seemed to take the time to make up her mind. Then she opened those beautiful golden eyes. "I want you, too."

He reached out and touched her hair. She tensed, but let him cup the back of her skull. He pulled her closer, smelled the floral scent of her light perfume. Her long black hair slid over his hands like silk. Most women in business wore their hair up but she never did, something he appreciated. He pulled her gently toward him and she took the step that he needed to know that this time she told the truth.

She wanted him.

What was she doing? Why was she letting him in? She couldn't tell him the truth except about how he affected her. And was that part of the change too? Would she have acted this way a few months ago? Was the desire she felt, the need, all a part of her curse?

What would happen if she let him…? No, not if she let him take her, what she felt was stronger than that. What if she took him? A part of her, a growing part, wanted to grab hold of him and roll them onto the floor right now. To growl and bite…

And then he was kissing her, his lips firm and warm against hers. She opened her mouth and tasted him. He tasted like he smelled, of brandy and man, and she wanted more, so much more.

He wrapped his other arm around her and pulled her close. She melted against the onslaught of his hands, his lips… It felt so good to be held, be desired. It had been too long and maybe it was worth the risk to have his embrace for a little while. She kissed him back and he must have felt the change in her because he gripped her tighter, pressing her tight to his body so she could feel the heat of him everywhere.

She ran her hands over the strong muscles of his arms and back. They were tense, as if he were poised for action.

Did he want her that much or did he already know that this was a bad idea? Did he have any clue about the danger he was in simply by being near her? She pulled her lips from his but didn't let him go. For a moment the only sound was their breathing. After a moment, he let her go and stepped away. She let him, although it was the exact opposite of what she wanted.

Stopping was the right thing to do. While it would be fun and a huge relief of tension, sex meant intimacies she wasn't able to share anymore. And even if she could get things sorted out on a personal level, they were going to be business partners. Business and pleasure never mixed well.

He turned back to her. "So, you aren't even going to tell the truth about this. There's a pull between us that could make things really, really good. You know it."

He'd stiffened, his shoulders rigid, and the corner of his mouth tilted down. He was right—she was lying. But how could she tell him the truth? In another week the change would become too difficult to control and she'd have to leave. Next month maybe, after she found the Rom and made them take their curse away, she'd be able to tell him something. He'd never believe what was happening to her now.

Hell, sometimes she didn't believe it.

She tried to clear things up. "We're going to be working together—"

"Maybe. Maybe not," he practically growled.

His frustration and desire heated the room and his scent had changed, growing sharper with frustration. His aggressive stance made her heart pound as much as his kiss had earlier and her bra suddenly seemed too tight. Her hands tingled and she glanced down. Her fingernails were darkening, sharpening. *Oh, God.*

"You have to go. I need you to go."

He took a step toward her. "Just tell me what is happening. What are you involved in? Are you in trouble? I can help—"

Tears threatened to fall and it was all she could do to hold them back. "You can't help." What could he do but complicate things further? She could fix this on her own, once she found those goddamn Gypsies. She pulled her shoulders back and lifted her chin, then walked to the door. She opened it and waited. After a moment he walked out but hesitated at the threshold.

"When you're ready to tell me the truth, I'll be ready to help you. Until then, I think business can wait." He walked to the elevator without looking back and she quietly shut the door.

She'd lost the deal for Multoma. No way would he work with them now on either project and it was all because of her. Promotion or not, she'd likely lose her job, her career. Everything she'd ever worked for would be gone and because of what? Because she'd done her job and some Gypsies got in the way.

Well, they were going to pay for it. After this change, she was going hunting. And before she exiled herself this time, she was going to discover just where her hunting territory would extend. She wiped away the tear that had managed to escape and picked up her briefcase. At least her claws had become nails again once David had left. The alpha strength of him had made her appreciate what that strength could do for her sexually, and that had brought on the beginning of her change as much as his aggression had. And wouldn't that be the end of any sexual adventure. *Sorry, David, you don't mind a little fur in the bed, do you? Care for a bite?*

She snorted, and then took a deep breath. At least she could still see a little humor in it all. Dark humor, to be sure, but what the hell, better than crying. She strode to her desk in her home office and unpacked her weapons—a powerful laptop and a top-of-the-line cell phone.

She'd begun the search for the Rom immediately after her first change, but this time she wouldn't be distracted by anything. Whatever they had done to her had to stop. Maybe it was magic…what the hell else could it be? So, she'd have to search that, too.

Hours ticked by until she forced herself to stop. Her stomach growled fiercely the moment she stood. She walked to the kitchen and opened the refrigerator. Not much inside had any appeal but she made herself a quick omelet. She considered her options as she got ready for bed. There was no way she would ever find a cure herself. The Rom had done this to her and they would have to fix her. But at least she had an idea of where to find them.

She climbed into bed and went to turn out the light. It wasn't on. She looked around the room. She could see as well now in the dark as she used to with the lights on. Another part of the curse that was just a tiny bit like a gift. What a mess. She closed her eyes fell back on the pillows.

Running. Running with soft pine needles beneath her feet. Wind in the air brought scents of the forest, and him. She grinned and raced past another tree, chasing her prey and gaining ground. The breeze tickled her sides and feathered through her hair. She laughed aloud and dug her bare toes deeper into the pine needles, pushing herself faster and faster as the chase was nearly over.

Then she was on him. She knocked him to the ground with a grunt and fell with him into a pile of dried leaves. They crunched beneath them as he twisted and flipped her and she reveled in the way his scent mixed with hers and the sharp scent of pine needles, the moldy smell of dried leaves. Sex in the woods like this with David was the best. First the chase, then the rough sex that pleased the beast inside her. They'd go for finesse later. She caught hold of his shoulder and bit him hard, drawing blood. The taste was heaven —sharp and powerful and invigorating. But he shouted and she jumped away from him in shock.

His eyes were wild. David. She smelled fear and growled, the sound low and deep. Was he afraid of her? Her heart seemed to drop into her stomach.

But his gaze had shifted to the woods around them. He wasn't looking at her at all and while relief was sweet, she turned to stare at the woods that suddenly seemed dark.

The shadows moved.

"Run!"

Helen threw off the covers and jumped to her feet. The urge to run brought panting gasps from her lungs. She shivered and ripples of sensation—goose bumps, each individual hair rising—raced over her skin. She glanced at her bed and found the sheets shredded. There was no more time. She needed to go now, not next week.

The change was coming.

Thank God for GPS. For the last two hours the road had become a narrow, twisting, single lane path amid a dense forest of trees. Not a house to be seen, let alone a convenience store or gas station. Good thing Helen was fully provisioned. Yesterday, when she'd put in for her leave, it was immediately approved. That never happened. She must've scared her boss more than she'd thought. How much of the change had he seen? Would she even have a job to go back to? She had the next two months—the entire eight weeks that she'd built up over the last two years by never taking a day off. The vacation time had grown without her noticing. Her life centered on work and nothing else— perfectly boring.

But she had plenty of excitement now, didn't she? The irony of it brought a half laugh to her lips.

Finally, she spotted the even smaller turn off, or at least she hoped this was it. The lane wasn't paved, basically just a graveled path in the woods. She'd driven for most of the day and it was getting darker now. Of course, the twilight meant little to her. Twenty minutes later, the gravel ran out and the path was nothing but two ruts. She bit her lip. If she couldn't find the place, she'd end up spending the night in her vehicle. The idea was unsettling, although she really didn't have a lot to fear these days. People maybe, and discovery, but not much else. If anyone found out what she'd become, she'd end up a dissection project in some mad scientist's laboratory.

The urge to turn around and find a way back to civilization was becoming insistent when she spotted a building in the shadows. This was it, and it was pretty much as she'd expected. Old, rarely used, and nearly abandoned. Nearly, because she knew David had been here a few months earlier. Gray cedar siding and a sagging porch with a roof, small windows and a good-sized chimney that made her long for a crackling fire. If David hadn't provided the coordinates of his father's old hunting camp in his proposal, she would've never found this spot.

She parked to one side of the cabin and sat in the SUV, staring out into the shadows. She would have to stay here for the next week and a half. Long enough to keep her secret, and prevent anyone from getting hurt, including her. Hopefully, there'd be a decent bed, although she'd picked up a sleeping bag and some basics at the camping goods outlet, just in case.

Well, nothing for it but to get out and unpack, move in no matter what conditions she found inside. The grass had grown tall around the old place. Luckily, she'd put on a pair of jeans for the trip and a T-shirt. She pulled on her light jacket—no point in getting bitten by mosquitoes and ticks— popped the trunk, and got out. With the car off the radio fell silent. The shadows had grown longer and she was struck by how very alone she was in this place. Alone was good. Alone was safe.

But it was still alone.

Two trips and she had all her supplies on the porch, which was more stable than it had looked. The screen door was boarded shut and padlocked, but a few sharp yanks took care of that and the lock gave way in her grip. She'd never considered herself very strong, but there was something satisfying in the way the metal folded under her fingers. Of course, that brought back thoughts of David and that damn fork.

What did he think of her? What would he imagine when he realized she was gone again? Would he tell anyone? Go to her boss and complain and mention the weird things he'd seen? No one would believe him. Except…she'd frightened Mr. Winfield. Still, people believed what they wanted to believe and Winfield was a pragmatic man, from her experience. She brought the company money, which should hold things in check for a little while.

The inner door wasn't locked and opened with only a light creak. Inside was dark even to her, so she pulled a flashlight from her pack and flicked it on.

At least here was a pleasant surprise. She hummed in pleasure. The cabin was fully furnished and had a beautiful fireplace. From the smell, someone—David—had lit a fire here not too many months ago. And although the place was a bit musty, nothing had rotted and no animals had gotten in. Her sense of smell could tell her a lot of things. David had been the only person here for some time.

She brought her things in, shut the door, and explored. Using the bedroom didn't feel right; sleeping in someone's bed was like she was taking too much of an advantage. The couch would do nicely and was near the fire so she'd be warm, although that wasn't much of an issue for her this time of the month. But at least the illusion of safety and hominess would be there for her. There was no power of course, but she had her solar charger for her lantern and phone, and a small cook stove and a cooler. It would keep things fresh enough until she didn't need to… She grimaced at the thought of hunting.

Sometimes she didn't need to worry about eating human food. Or at least nothing that had to be cooked. Or gutted. Or even deboned.

She pressed her lips tightly together and got busy putting things away neatly. David might intend on leveling this place, but someone had loved it once. There were signs everywhere, including the handmade rock fireplace and the family photos on the mantle above it. She lit a small fire—there was plenty of wood stacked to one side of the fireplace, and she'd discovered a small room at the back that contained at least a cord of dry wood.

One of the photos on the mantle was of David and an older man with similar features. It had to be his father. David was a young man, maybe twenty, and they were laughing. His father had an arm wrapped around David's shoulders.

She had no similar photo with her father. He'd never been the hugging kind, or the laughing kind, that she could remember. She turned away. Clearly, she was getting over-tired. Sentimentality was a complete waste of time. She unrolled her sleeping bag, plopped down her pillow on the end of the couch and tugged a book out of her kit. With nothing else to do, at least she'd be cutting down her 'to be read' pile.

She'd done it again. She was gone and no one had a clue where she'd gone. Eight fucking weeks? She'd booked eight weeks off and disappeared. What the hell?

David paced his office. *Goddammit.* This was his fault. He'd told her business could wait until she was ready to tell him the truth. Clearly she wasn't and his trying to force her had pushed her to leave, maybe earlier than she'd planned. But he still had no idea where she was or why she kept taking off. And what about their deal?

He paced back to his desk and dropped into the chair. Maybe this was a sign. He should just back off and find another developer. There were other companies he could work with. Multoma had been his first choice and it could have taken him to a whole new level, made his small company a much stronger one. Now the project would have to wait. And the spa retreat? He'd leave that off the drawing board. He never should have told her anything about it.

His stomach burned. It was hard to say who he was angrier with—her for leaving, or him, for telling her too much. Sharing his idea when he hadn't even bought all the surrounding land. Yes, he had a good bit of the property secured on the mountain, but not all of it. She'd been so interested. Wanted all the details.

He sat up straight. What had she said? She'd asked a lot of questions about the land, specifically his father's old cabin. And before, she'd tried to claim that she'd been investigating land for development when she'd taken off. Could that part have been true? He'd been sure she was lying, but maybe not entirely. What if she'd gone there, to the cabin to check out the mountain while she did whatever she did when she escaped work and the city?

It was long shot, but it was the only thing he could think of. She wasn't the type to steal his development; he was a good enough judge of character to believe that. But what if she bought the land around it? That was possible. Then she'd be part owner, or Multoma would be, depending on whose behalf she was really acting.

He leaned back in his chair. Something didn't really fit. He'd already decided she wasn't crooked; she worked for her company and herself but wasn't likely to cheat him out of anything. He trusted his instincts; they'd never steered him wrong. His instincts said she was in trouble.

He called her secretary. They'd left on much better terms than they'd begun, when he'd barged into Helen's office. "Hello, Sherry. I know you said Helen wasn't in, but I'm wondering if she did or said anything yesterday that might give you any clue as to where she's gone?

"No, I'm sorry, Mr. Sherman. She put in for her leave, wrapped up a few things, and left."

There had been a slight hesitation before Sherry had said Helen left. She knew something but did she trust David with it? "I'm worried about her, Sherry. I think you're worried too. There must have been something."

The hesitation was longer this time. "Well, she did make arrangements to take a cab to Cabela's, that big hunting and camping superstore. That was unusual."

"Thanks, Sherry."

"But, Mr. Sherman, please, she's always been wonderful to work for. It's only been in the last little bit that things have been off, and she looks so stressed, so tired. If you aren't going to help her, don't get involved."

"I'm going to help. Thank you." He hung up. He was already involved, his interest piqued, and something inside him told him she could be something very special. How could he not try to help her?

Cabela's wasn't far from the outskirts of the city. He could be there in twenty minutes with the light traffic at this time of day. And if she were after the kind of camping gear that he suspected, then his idea about where she could be headed might be true. A few minutes with the sales-people who had been on duty the day before would be enough to let him know. Who would be able to forget a perfectly dressed business woman, a beautiful one, coming in for camping gear and probably asking all sorts of questions?

He'd go home, pack his own gear, and then head over to the store. If he was right, he'd head for the hunting cabin and catch up with her there and find out what was wrong. But, if he wasn't right and she wasn't there, well, it had been a while since he'd seen the old cabin or taken a vacation.

Considering the crazy ideas he'd been having about what could be going on with Helen, maybe he needed one.

***

Helen stuck her bookmark in her novel and dropped the book with a sigh. Last night had been cozy in the cabin and she'd slept well enough on the couch. In the morning she'd spent a good bit of time figuring out the camp stove and making a light brunch, but after a day with nothing but her books, the boredom might soon kill her. Time to go out. She'd had no signs of the change since she'd arrived; obviously she was free of the stress that had been bringing them on early. The stress from one particular man and all his questions.

She stood and paced. There were only a few days left until the change would become too strong to resist. She stopped and stared out the window at the forest. She could bring the change on now by going into the woods and simply let it happen. She'd never done that before. Never consciously brought it on or tried to control it, only tried to stop it. It was in the back of her mind, always, nagging at her to let go and let it happen.

There was new growth out there in the woods near the cabin, mixed with old, old trees. Enough leaf cover above that the brush was thin underneath the canopy only a few yards past the first trees. She could walk out there, strip off her clothes, and feel the breeze on her skin. It wasn't cold, not really, and never to her. She wouldn't be naked for long, but for a few minutes she'd be exposed. She shivered. There was something exciting about the idea, although she'd never considered the change to be sensual at all. That part hurt a bit, though not as much as she'd imagined from watching movies. Blood and bone changing shape, senses sharpening, the power of sudden strength…these things should have been accompanied by agony. But the pain was more like an awakening.

Would bringing the change on be like giving into it? Would it make things harder next time when she wanted to stop it? Would she lose control? Lose herself to the other? She bit her lip and paced the room again. This was the argument that she'd had several times with herself already today.

Maybe changing early would make it easier to stop later. This was the flip side of the debate. Maybe if she got to know this thing better, understand herself after the change, she could control it longer, and change only when she wanted. Like she'd ever *want* to. She'd have to deal with it until she dealt with the Rom and made them remove the curse.

"Control is power, Helen. Get used to that." Her father never let go of his control. Not up until the day he died, although if he had, they might have realized his little headaches were a sign of something far worse. So, yeah, he hadn't always been right. Was he right now? If she had control over the change, would she be more powerful?

She'd have to be.

She took a deep breath and headed for the door. She hesitated for a second then slipped outside, leaving the inner door open and the just the screen door shut to let in some air. At times during the night, the faint scent of David had been enough to wake her from dreams that seemed too impossible, yet were also real.

The tall grass brushed at her knees as she walked across the overgrown yard to the woods. She breathed deeply. The smells here were fantastic, so fresh and alive. The grass, new and old. The loamy ground beneath it. The trees ahead, most with big green leaves and some with dark needles, none of which she could name but she definitely could smell. And the exciting scents of little animals—mice, squirrels, rabbits. She licked her lips.

Now that she had made up her mind she was going to do this, it seemed so easy. Her nails were already hardening, growing longer and darker. She cocked her head at a small sound, but it was only a few birds, crows maybe, gathering to perch in the trees nearby. Were they watching her? She had to laugh at herself. They were only birds.

She grabbed the edge of her T-shirt and pulled it over her head. The breeze tickled her skin just as she'd imagined. She quickly folded her shirt and laid it on a flat rock. She looked back. She could still see the house. It was so simple to step out of her shoes. To pull off her socks and pull down her jeans. She folded them and laid them beside the shirt. Her bra and underwear were a little harder. She bit her lip as the breeze tickled her everywhere, as attentive as any lover.

She could feel the change hovering, just off the point of actualization. Sometimes it seemed as if it had always been there, waiting to pounce, to bring her into a world so different from her day-to-day life.

One deep breath, a moment of relaxation, and it was on her. She shifted in moments, her skin and bones forming a new shape, one filled with power and strength. The pain was there, unsurprising and yet somehow less than usual. Was this because she wasn't fighting it? Because she'd let it happen? If that was the case the experiment was so far bringing positive results.

Her senses opened; the sights and sounds and smells

became so much stronger. The vegetation beneath her feet was too hard to resist and she rolled in it, stretching and scratching her new body. Then she was up and off, running. Even when she'd fought the change there was nothing better than those first hours, when she ran and ran, stretching like she'd been cramped in her office for years.

Which she had.

Twilight had settled in and the forest was open to her. She'd been right—there was little scrub under the largest part of the canopy and the speed she brought on made her giggle. God only knew what that sounded like. She let her tongue loll out and tasted the air. There was so much life around her, so much freedom before her.

It was too bad that David intended to develop this land. Running here was the best she'd found. That thought brought her run to an end. She slowed. Accepting the change was dangerous after all. How easy it would be to make this her life. This freedom. She'd lose everything she'd built—her career. And then what would she do when she was herself? When she was human and her reason for getting up every morning was gone?

A strange scent wafted past her, and her hackles drew up. Predator. More than one. And close. She scanned the shadows, and a flicker of movement drew her attention to the left. Then it was gone, and a hint of motion caught her peripheral vision on the other side. *Danger.*

A howl soared through the air, carrying threat and promise like a deadly song. She raced again, running back the way she came, back toward David's cabin. Then it hit her, a wave of otherness, a power she felt like a cold wave of water, hitting her and knocking her off balance. She stumbled, fell, and screamed as her body tore open and her human form was yanked into the open in a bloody, pain-filled instant.

For a second she lay dazed on the ground.

Then the howl came again, joined by a second voice, and a third. A chorus of animal and human mixed together and her heart dropped into her belly.

She got up, and she ran.

7

David's headlights cut through the darkness, but they never did much on this part of the mountain other than make him feel claustrophobic. Why the hell was he doing this? Curiosity he could understand—that was a feeling he'd followed often both as a child and as a man, and it often led him toward good things. And yes, he'd admit he had a serious attraction for a mystery and Helen Mathews was definitely that. Not to mention beautiful and he'd always had a weakness for a beautiful woman.

But had he ever gone after a woman with this kind of intense need to help? Nope. That was a new one for him. She needed him. Whatever was going on, he could feel it. And maybe, that was it. His mother called him a good man, and his brothers called him Boy Scout. So, there was that.

He could count on his hands the last time he'd chased a woman. Yet here he was chasing after the mysterious and needy Helen. What did that say about him? That he needed to be needed. No kidding. The last time anyone had needed him was Sharon. That had ended badly. She'd needed what he couldn't give—a way back to reality. She'd had psychological problems he'd known nothing about and in the end, had taken her own life. He knew it wasn't his fault, wasn't anyone's fault, but… He hadn't been able to protect her no matter how much he cared for her.

"No wonder you've been hanging out with simple, curvy blondes," he muttered. And now he was self analyzing as he drove halfway up a mountain after a woman who might not be there, and might not want him around if she was.

"It's my bloody place, for God's sake." He'd be at the turn off soon, just a little farther. "You're talking to yourself." He shook his head and then slammed on the brakes as a figure dashed into the road ahead of him. "Jesus Christ!"

The figure, a woman, naked and bloody, switched direction and ran straight up the road. Helen. For a second his mind flashed back to the dream he'd had recently. But this was reality. He put his Jeep in park and opened the door, shouted her name. She faltered slightly, but kept running.

"Goddammit!" He slammed the door and ran after her, leaving the engine running.

She ran like the wind, like death was chasing her. What had happened? Had she been attacked? He'd been in track in university and had kept up his running since then, but he had to give it everything he had to catch up to her. He grabbed her by the elbow and she jerked in his grasp, and stumbled.

"Helen, stop!"

"They're coming! We've got to run—"

"Who? Are you hurt? Whose blood is this?"

"Mine." Her eyes were wild. He grabbed her again and tried to check for wounds but she squirmed away. "We have to go!"

She was losing it, the fear in her eyes uncontrolled. A hundred questions flooded his mind, but first things first; he had to get her somewhere safe. "Come on then, my car is back on the road."

Her gaze darted to the woods and she struggled harder to get free of him. "Can't go back. They're coming. The wolves."

He frowned and his heart pounded harder than it had from the run. There were no wolves on the mountain. None in the state that he knew of. Was she having a mental break? "Come with me, Helen. You're okay now. You're safe. Let's take my car back to the cabin." He spoke soothingly, keeping his tone gentle. Someone must have attacked her and she was somehow associating the attack with the most frightening image she could think of, wolves.

She stared at him for a second, really focusing in on him for the first time since he'd caught up with her. "You go back to your car. Maybe they won't do anything to you. They're after me."

She sounded in control. But wolves? David and Helen were both breathing heavily and the chill in the air formed a fog from their breath. It brought his attention back to the fact that she was naked in the cold fall air. Wherever all the blood was coming from, she didn't seem to have any major wounds that he could see. Not that he was staring. He let her go for a moment and pulled off his jacket. He put it over her shoulders and turned her around toward the car, where he could see the headlights glowing.

He looked back at her but pointed down the road. "Look, see my car? Let's just go back, get in, and drive to the cabin. We can get you cleaned up and we can figure out what happened and if we should call the police."

She looked at him, trembled. Fear radiated from her, and a little shiver slid down his spine.

They both looked at the glowing headlights. They blinked out.

"What?" He couldn't have lost battery power already. He'd barely let the thing idle a few minutes. A moment later he realized he could still hear the engine. In fact it was roaring. Toward them.

"Run! They've got your car!" Helen grabbed his hand, dragged him along with her while she ran up the road toward the cabin. His jacket slipped from her shoulders and fell to the ground as her long strides ate up the ground and he ran with her.

"Who? Who is it?"

"The wolves! Now run!" She veered into the woods and he followed. The car roared closer, then past, a waft of air rushing over them in its wake.

"Wolves have my car?" The woman ran like the wind and he could barely keep up and get the words out. But disbelief at the whole situation raced even faster through his mind. He jumped a fallen log. He could barely see now they were off the road, but the nearly full moon gave just enough light to keep them moving. Something terrible had happened to Helen, or was still happening. She needed help, but maybe more than he could give her, because somebody had his car. He could get her somewhere safe, but then she would need professional help. The police and a doctor. She was suffering from delusions.

The cabin wasn't far now, but David was slowing them down. She couldn't leave him out in the woods, the dark, not really understanding who was after them or how much danger he was in. They might not be after him, but they'd taken his car. Whoever they were, they were cursed like her. Shifting forms to hunt her in as both human and wolf. She knew they wanted her, had sensed their hostility before she'd changed back, but who were they? Why did they want to hurt her?

She'd find out later. Right now she needed to get David safe inside, before he got deeper into trouble. That had to be why he was here. He'd come after her, too curious to stay away. She pulled on his arm and he grunted and poured on a little speed. They were getting close.

The sound of David's Jeep grew stronger. The wolves had turned around on the road and were rushing back toward them. "They're coming back!"

This time David jerked on her arm. He pulled them deeper into the woods as the Jeep crashed through the bush only yards from where they'd been. She glanced over her shoulder. The Jeep was lodged between trees, unable to go deeper into the woods after them. The lights were still out but she could see the driver through the front window. A man with a snarl on his face—a stranger whose teeth were growing longer every second.

David led them deeper into the trees. "Where are we going?" she yelled.

"Shortcut," he panted. "Come on."

They ran.

Long minutes later they burst into the relatively clear area around the cabin. There'd been no sign of the wolves, no hint of their hunting howl. No sound of anything at all. The night was eerily silent. What did they say in the movies? Quiet—too quiet. Every second she expected them to burst from the shadows of the trees and fling themselves on her, ripping her to shreds.

They pounded across the lawn and up the stairs of the cabin porch. David staggered and she pulled him upright and to the door. He pulled the screen door open and then burst inside. She slammed the door shut behind them, and slapped the bolt across. For a moment they stood there, panting. David bent over and pressed his palms to his knees while he did his best to breathe. Then she rushed to the widow and peered outside.

The night stayed quiet.

A small sound caught her attention. David had recovered enough to walk to the table beside the sofa. He opened a drawer and pulled out a set of keys. Then he grabbed the blanket off the sofa that she'd been using as a bed and came to her. He looked away as he handed her the wool cover and she flushed as she took it and covered herself. "Thank you." The words came from her in a tone she barely recognized as her own. Soft, quavering.

He nodded. He looked like he wanted to say something to her, or maybe he was waiting for her to speak first. His eyes searched hers. But what could she say to him? How could she explain this mess? He was in danger because he'd followed her. She glanced at the floor.

He sighed and walked away, toward the direction of the master bedroom. She stared after him, and then returned her stare to the window. Who was out there? Why had they attacked her? What had they done to change her back so suddenly? Had they somehow taken the curse from her?

"I'm sure they've gone, or they would have been at the cabin by now." David had returned and stood behind her. She changed her focus and looked at him in the reflection of the window. Then she turned and looked at him for real. He held a shotgun and a box of shells. "Just in case they come back."

She raised her eyebrows.

"What? This is a hunting cabin." He grinned at her and she giggled, but the noise quickly began to sound hysterical.

He frowned and set the shell box down, reached out to touch her shoulder. "Are you hurt?"

She looked down at herself. Was she hurt? How could she not know? She looked down at her arm and was surprised at the amount of blood covering it. There was blood everywhere. And now that she could see it, she could smell it. The coppery tang of her own life. "Just…just scratches I think. I… I…"

"We should call the police."

"No! No, I don't want them. I'm okay."

A small muscle jumped along his jaw. He rubbed his thumb over her collarbone through the blanket. "Why don't you get cleaned up and dressed. I'll keep watch. And then you can tell me what happened, okay?"

He was treating her like she was wounded, or maybe as a child. It felt ridiculously good to listen to him, and to agree. She shivered. Silently, she picked up her bag and walked to the bathroom. Inside, she faced the shock of her appearance in the full length mirror behind the door. She gasped.

There really was blood everywhere—in her hair, on her face. She dropped the blanket. Everywhere. What could David possibly imagine happened to her? That she'd been attacked? Raped? She'd told him wolves were chasing her and he hadn't believed it. And then they'd stolen his car. Showed her who they were, or at least what. And she'd seen one face, one she wouldn't forget.

She turned away from her reflection. The scent of blood sickened her. She stepped into the shower and turned it on, only flinching once at the stinging cold. The water ran red at her feet. There were no scratches anywhere on her. No place for the blood to have come from but the change.

They had literally ripped her human form from inside the wolf.

She ached; the muscles in her legs and back and pretty much everywhere else throbbed with dull pain. The cold water wasn't helping, so she shut it off and toweled herself dry. A few minutes later she was wrapped in a towel, but still in the bathroom. Going back out to the main room meant facing David and all his questions. What was she supposed to tell him? She'd seen his expression when she said it was wolves chasing them. He thought she'd lost her sanity. But if she avoided him much longer, his protective nature would kick in and he'd call the cops or so something similarly stupid, like assume the wolves were gone and go out to look at his damaged vehicle.

She closed her eyes.

Maybe it was over. Maybe, by pulling her from the wolf, they'd stopped her from changing again. But then why were they so intent on hurting her? They'd tried to kill her and David with the Jeep.

She licked her lips. Other than tonight, she'd never tried to actively allow the change to take place. Did that have something to do with the attack? She stared at her hands, willing the nails to shift into claws, always the first sign that she was losing control and the change was coming. Nothing.

Her heartbeat picked up. Could it really be over?

A knock sounded on the door and she jumped.

"Helen?" David's voice carried a strong note of concern. "Are you okay in there?"

She went to the door and opened it. David looked her over carefully from head to toe. His concern was sweet, if misguided.

"Do you need some bandages? The first aid kit is in the kitchen. I can go get it for you."

"No, I'm fine."

He frowned. "Then where did all the blood come from, Helen?"

She leaned against the door and sighed. "You wouldn't believe me."

He shook his head, turned and walked away from her, back to the living room where he set the shotgun on the coffee table and took a seat on the sofa. He called out to her.

"If you don't explain this to me in five minutes, I'm calling the cops. And please, put some clothes on."

Heat flushed through her. She slammed the door shut, yanked out some clothes from her bag, and hurriedly dressed. No time to comb her hair. She was going to have to tell him something, but what?

She rushed out to the living room and dropped into the recliner opposite the couch. He had his phone out, sitting beside the shotgun on the table. *Yippee, a showdown.*

For a minute they sat there, staring at each other. Then he started to reach for the phone.

"Okay, all right. Don't call the police. But you really aren't going to believe me." Helen rushed through the words, but when he leaned back in the couch again, away from his cell, she stalled.

"I'm listening." His voice was deep. Neutral, with maybe a hint of concern. Well, who wouldn't be concerned? He found her covered in blood, which he probably figured wasn't hers, and then someone tried to run them down with his own vehicle. Helen fidgeted and bit her lip.

He raised an eyebrow.

She leaned forward and rested her forearms against her thighs. "You're going to think I've lost my mind. Sometimes, I think it. It all started with the hospital project. There was this group of people…wanderers. Gypsies. They call themselves the Rom. From Romania, I guess. I've tried to research them, but there isn't much. They didn't own the land, or any rights to it. I didn't do anything wrong."

"That old woman—"

"Yes, that damn woman." She looked up at him, caught the way he was staring at her, interested, concerned. As if he really cared. She swallowed hard. Why would he? "She did it. Bianca Donceanu. She's a lawyer, apparently, but she's something more to her people. They didn't have a leg to stand on in court so she showed up at my company's award ceremony and ruined me."

"She embarrassed you. But ruined?"

Helen looked away. "She cursed me. Threw some sort of spell at me. I told you, she's something more than a lawyer. They use the land as they travel across several states each year. But I took it and made it into something better than a campground. And they didn't appreciate it." She fell silent. The memory of blood splashing across her, all the company staring, the strange feeling that came with the witch's words…

"What do you mean, curse? And was it people from the Rom chasing you tonight?"

Helen closed her eyes. This was the part where he'd not only call the cops, but call the medics to come with a nice white straightjacket. "I'm sure it was them. Why they were here tonight, and not before, I don't know. The curse. It changes me. I have to leave, go somewhere where no one can see, and no one can get hurt. This is the third time. The moon becomes full, and I become a beast. A…wolf. A werewolf."

She looked at him. Yup, she'd lost him. He looked back at her with disbelief and worse, pity.

"Helen, we have to call for help. You need help."

She stood, paced the room. "Really. Really? You saw them. They're after me. I don't know why, after months of being like this, but they were here last night and they did something. They…" She couldn't find the words. "Something magic. It's where the blood came from. From me, but not from my skin, not this skin…" She wasn't making sense and she could see he believed she'd really lost it.

"I twisted that fork, remember? I'm stronger now. Faster, and I can see and hear better. Smell better. But you think I'm nuts."

He stood and reached out to her but she paced away. "I think you are in trouble. Something is definitely going on, and those people did chase us, but a werewolf? No. You are not a beast of any kind."

Frustration ate at her. He made perfect sense. Stuff like this couldn't be real. And yet it was. She'd been living it. She growled and the sound came out as animalistic as what she'd heard from the wolves in the woods.

"I am a beast." She held up her hands. The nails that had refused to shift earlier were blackening, lengthening as she watched. Her teeth felt longer, sharper. He had to know what she was, but showing him the change seemed horrible in reality. He would be repulsed at the shift, the way her bones cracked and moved, the way the fur sprouted from her skin and she became other. It could only be an ugly thing, unnatural. Unclean.

Already her hands were changing, and the ache was becoming severe in her legs and arms. She dashed past him to the door, pushing him aside. He grunted in surprise and she made it to the door before he could see it all.

"Helen, wait!"

But she was gone, running as pain flashed through her body and the change took place, slower than normal, but unstoppable. What choice did she have but to run from him? Even if the wolves waited for her in the woods, it was better than being here with a man who only wanted to help—a man she would surely hurt.

8

"What. The hell. Was. That?" David breathed. What had just happened? How could he possibly have seen what he had just seen? Helen Mathews, beautiful Helen, was in the process of becoming a werewolf.

"No. No way." David sat back down on the couch with a thump and stared at the open doorway.

Long minutes ticked by while he tried to wrap his mind around everything he knew about Helen. She'd had an altercation with a strange woman at her promotion dinner. She'd gone missing every few weeks since it happened. She could bend a fork as easily as crashing a wad of paper. And her eyes were a color he'd only ever seen in one other place—in the wolf print on his bedroom wall.

Something else he knew—someone had been chasing her. She was afraid; none of the fear coming from her tonight had been a lie. Now she was back out there, running in the woods because either she couldn't handle him seeing her shift, or because she thought once she did, she might hurt him. Either way she had run to the same woods they'd escaped from only a couple of hours earlier. The people chasing them, wolves or not, could still be out there. He glanced at his watch. Twenty minutes past midnight. Jesus. He'd been sitting, visiting la-la land for more than an hour, while she'd been out there alone.

He got up and after a moment's hesitation grabbed the shotgun. He pocketed as many shells as he could and walked to the door. She still needed him. Maybe. She had been coated in blood earlier. While she'd said it was hers, what if it had been someone else's? What if it had been from a victim, another person? But then what if it had been from a fight, self defense? They hadn't gotten far enough to ask. He'd just assumed she was suffering from a mental breakdown, just as Sharon had on the one weekend he'd ignored her calls.

Guilt. It would never leave him. And he wasn't about to add the weight of more guilt now. He'd either stop Helen from hurting anyone, or stop anyone from hurting her. He strode out the door, shutting the screen behind him.

Unlike before, clouds now obscured some of the light from the moon. A cool breeze wafted through the trees and scattered dried leaves, making soft skittering noises. The hair on the back of his neck lifted. "This is likely the stupidest thing you've ever done trying to help someone, Sherman. And there've been some doozies," he muttered under his breath.

He took a few steps into the trees and called her name. "Helen!"

Nothing.

Then, a long howl lifted into the night sky, a sound that rose and fell with a primordial eeriness that sent his heart thundering. No other voices joined the chorus, but one was quite enough.

"Holy fuck..." he breathed. He stepped backward, out of the trees, carefully walking back into the tall grass clearing next to the cabin.

When he backed up far enough to feel the edge of the wooden steps to the cabin behind him he stopped, loaded the gun. At the edge of the woods a form appeared. The clouds parted, and he stopped breathing.

A wolf. A real wolf when such a thing hadn't been seen on this mountain in his lifetime or his father's. But was it a real wolf? The creature was huge and bright, its fur nearly white when he thought most wolves were gray.

He swallowed hard. The wolf took a few steps into the clearing. It stared at him, ears perked forward. He stared back. Then, very carefully, without turning his back, he walked up the stairs to the cabin, went in and shut the door. Locked it. Leaned against it and tried to breathe.

After a moment he went to the window. The wolf still watched, but now it was pacing forward. It reached the cabin, leaped to the top of the stairs, and then sat facing the woods. The woods, not him. It was even bigger than he'd thought. *She* was even bigger. He leaned his gun against the wall. He'd never even pointed it toward her. He knew who he faced.

Who she was.

And now she was standing guard on the cabin. He ran a hand through the back of his hair, felt the cold sweat there. Well, she could stand guard outside. He might know who she was, but she could stay on the other side of the door, thanks. Hard to say if she knew for sure who he was, when she was like this.

He looked out the window again. She looked over her shoulder at him with those golden eyes. He'd been right. She was no beast. She was magnificent, a powerful creature of the night. Beautiful. Deadly?

The moon sank and the woods grew dark, but nothing stirred. The local wildlife kept themselves far from the cottage and the predator lounging on the porch. The other wolves didn't return as she'd feared they might. And from inside the cottage? Nothing moved once David tended the fire for the night and settled himself on the couch. When the sun finally crept up on the horizon, Helen shifted again, her wolf withdrawing while her humanity returned.

She shivered, naked on the porch. Her wolf side hadn't wanted to leave, and she had to admit she felt distinctly vulnerable without the protection of claw and fang. At last she didn't have to bang on the cabin door and beg David for her clothes. She'd left her SUV unlocked and thankfully, she kept a blanket folded on the back seat, along with a small pillow. She walked over, climbed inside, and locked the doors. Moments after she tucked the blanket around her, she sank into sleep.

A sharp rapping on the window at her feet brought Helen awake. David stood outside the car, still dressed in yesterday's clothes and still carrying the shotgun. Was a shotgun even any good against werewolves? Weren't they only killed by silver bullets? She closed her eyes to think about that, and maybe sleep some more but he rapped on the window again.

"Helen, come out. There's breakfast."

His voice was gruff and he had the gun, but he wasn't freaking out and he was asking her in. She gripped the blanket and sat up. His eyes widened, probably realizing she was naked under it, and he stepped away from the SUV and walked back to the cabin.

Helen climbed out of her vehicle and stretched while making a rough toga with the car blanket. Last night's events played through her mind. The way she'd accepted her change and let it happen, then the attack and the forced shift back to human. For a little while she'd not been able to change back and thinking about it, she had to admit to herself that she'd been half afraid what they had done to her had been permanent. But the wolves hadn't come back, hadn't attacked her. Had David seen them?

Only one way to know. Plus, he knew her secret now. Was he going to tell anyone? Would anyone even believe him? The last thing she needed was to be locked up somewhere while someone tried to figure out what she was.

She followed David to the cabin. For a moment she stood in the doorway and watched him as he plated up some beans, eggs and strange looking, round toast. Where had he gotten the food? Had she been so exhausted she missed him leaving? No, his Jeep was likely out of commission for the foreseeable future.

He spotted her hesitating at the screen door. "Come in, I won't bite." He lifted his eyebrows. "And I expect you to behave and not bite, either."

A joke. The man managed to produce a full meal out of nothing *and* a joke after last night? She'd been right about him, he was strong.

"I leave some dried supplies here, canned bread and powdered eggs and stuff, in the hunting packs in the bedroom closet in case we stay out overnight on a hunt. I haven't taken anyone hunting in a while, but the stuff lasts for years. It's not bad," he added when she didn't move, and he took a big bite.

Her stomach grumbled and her mouth watered over the big pile of eggs on her plate. She walked in and took a seat at one of the stools beside the kitchen counter. He stayed on the other side, eating his breakfast while standing. He might be offering a meal, but he wasn't totally comfortable with her yet. Who could blame him?

She dug in, though she could feel his eyes on her, evaluating. It was awkward, eating with one hand while she kept a tight grip on the blanket with the other, but waiting for the food while she took the time to get dressed wasn't happening. They ate silently, until she was dipping the last of her toast into cooling tea.

David cleared his throat. "Tell me again how this happened. Make me believe I'm not crazy."

"You aren't going to call the police? Or the Navy? Local witchdoctor?" She tried to joke, but it was a bit past her acting abilities.

He shook his head. "No." He didn't have an ounce of humor in his tone.

She bit her lip. She owed him for coming up here after her, and trying to help. For possibly putting himself in danger. She told him about the land deal, this time in detail, about how the Rom used it for their annual migration but owned none of it; how they claimed they'd had a centuries old deal with the government; how a woman who first appeared as a crisp professional lawyer showed up and threw blood on her as part of a curse.

David poured her another cup of tea and a cup of coffee for himself when she faltered in the telling of her first change. The pain of it, the strangeness, the disbelief, and the damage she'd done to her apartment and to herself. Her neighbors had complained about the noise and about her having an animal. She'd left the next day to an old and empty campground she'd visited as a child, but the damage was done.

She sipped the tea. He'd remembered she didn't like coffee.

She told him of the exponential increase in her strength, speed, senses. Her pain at the touch of silver. For a moment she wondered why she'd revealed that fact, but really couldn't imagine him hurting her. Somehow, she'd wanted to trust him from the first moment she'd laid eyes on him, and that wasn't like her at all. She told him that, too.

"Why do you think that is?" he asked. He hadn't asked much, just watched her and listened.

Might as well go all in. She looked down at the empty plate until he took it away. Then she looked at her tea—anywhere but at him. This was *not* going to sound right. "It's how you smell, I think."

He leaned a little closer and she smelled him, that same strong woodsy scent of his cologne and the subtler scent that was his skin. Delicious. Warm. Honest. Her senses analyzed him and sent the results straight to her heart and her libido. She could trust him. She still wanted him. And maybe, he still wanted her.

"How do I smell?" His voice was deeper. The interest was still there. But he'd have to be crazy to act on it. Still, for just a minute she imagined being with him and how good it would be to be held, to be taken, to have nothing to think about but physical enjoyment for even a little while, rather than the craziness her life had become.

She clenched her jaw. She wouldn't feel sorry for herself. Never once had her father let her get away with that, not even when her mother died when she was little. And maybe that was a good thing. Sure, she'd perhaps gone too far with work, making it the center of her life, but right now, she needed the stiff spine he'd forced her to build. Otherwise how would she survive?

David came around the counter. "Helen, how do I smell to you?"

She looked up at him. The urge to growl was there, a pressure inside that had to be coming from the wolf. "You smell good. Like someone I can trust."

"Is that all?"

She licked her lips. Admit it or not? What the hell, he was all grown up and he could decide for himself if being with her was a risk he was willing to take. "Your scent…it makes me want you."

He reached out and stroked her hair. It must look a mess, but his fingers tangling in the long strands made her shiver and reminded her she wore only the car blanket toga.

He remembered it too. He touched the skin on her shoulders. "No blood this time, when you shifted."

"There isn't usually any. That was from whatever the other wolves did, pulling me back into human form somehow." He didn't stop touching and she leaned into his hand.

"Does it hurt? To shift?" He put his other hand on her as well, holding the sides of her face so he could look deep into her eyes.

"Yes. No," she murmured. Was he hypnotizing her? Pulling all the truth from her? "Not really. There's pain, but I found out if I don't fight it, it's…not bad. And once I am changed, there's strength and power…"

He moved a little closer. "But they hurt you."

"Yes—"

He kissed her, long, delicious movements against her lips until she stood and pressed against him, opening her mouth to let him in. He took it deeper and she let him lead. Let everything go and just followed where he wanted to take her. The relief of it appealed nearly as much as the strength of his arms as he pulled her in close, held her.

It wasn't enough. She wanted comfort, yes, but she'd wanted *him* from the moment she'd laid eyes on him. She'd been so tired that day, and he'd been so goddamned pushy, but still he'd brought on a level of desire she couldn't remember ever repeating. With a quick tug she dropped the blanket to the floor.

He pulled back, his face registering surprise in the lift of his eyebrows and the tiny gasp that left his lips. "Are you sure? You've been through a lot. Maybe we shouldn't push things too fast."

"I just want you, David. Isn't that enough? I know what I want and I want sex, now, with you. I'm not hurt, I'm not confused, and I'm not crazy."

He dropped his lips to hers again and delved deep, his tongue dipping inside to taste her in a way that made her long for more. Then he swept her from her feet and into his arms. Need washed over her and she leaned in to nuzzle his neck. He stumbled slightly over the dropped blanket and her teeth grazed his skin harder than she meant.

"No biting."

Likely a good idea, so she murmured a quick "sorry," and tugged his head down for a kiss. They made it to the bedroom but not before he knocked over an old vase of dried flowers on a side table beside the door. Finally he dropped her onto the bedspread.

"Helen…God, you're beautiful." He leaned down and stroked her hair, his fingers tangling in the strands. His body spoke silently of the tension it held within—his jaw clenched and the cords of muscle in his forearms stretched taut.

Full-blown lust. That was the only way to describe the sensation flooding his body. She looked like his favorite dreams transformed into life. She sat still on the mattress, one hand in his. Her hair was a cascade around her. Her face was flushed, both from her earlier frustration and her reaction to the words he had uttered. And her skin, so pure it glowed, made him want to leave bite marks. Hardly fair, since he'd just told her she couldn't bite him.

Was he an idiot for acting this way? Probably, but if she didn't say something soon, he was going to lose all control.

To hell with it—she was too beautiful not to at least kiss some more. He lowered himself to the bed, never taking his eyes away from hers. He held her gaze and leaned slowly forward, tilting his head to slant his lips against hers. He couldn't bring himself to shutter those light golden eyes from his view, and he watched as they glowed with a need to match his own.

He ran his hands over her, exploring. Still her eyes stayed open, and he deepened their kiss, running his tongue over her lips and separating them. Finally, he delved inside her mouth, tasting her sweetness. As he did she made a soft sound deep in her throat, and her eyes drifted closed. Was it surrender? It was so much more, he realized as she moved her own hands to run up his sides, stroking his back and coming to clutch at his shoulders.

For the briefest moment, he remembered the possible danger they were in. There could literally be wolves at the door. He should stop. Then, as she pulled closer to him, pressing upward against his body and striving to pull his waist closer, everything was forgotten except her.

She was perfect. Her skin was pale cream, smooth, flawless. Her breasts were small but the nipples were taut, jutting up at him like twin offerings. Impossible to resist. He lowered his mouth to her and dragged his lips over her skin.

Blood thundered through his veins as he struggled to take the moment slowly. When he sucked one nipple into his mouth he heard her moan, a low, powerful sound that God must have given women to drive men crazy. Between that, the scent of her, and the feeling of her supple skin under his hands and mouth, he might lose his mind.

When her hands stroked lower to rub at his thighs and the bulge in his jeans, he knew he was lost. A deep groan resonated in his throat. He raised his face to hers once more, and kissed her. As he held her he lowered her to the bed, and twisted to slide his legs onto the mattress. He levered on top of her, and rested part of his weight on her. He was never going to last if he didn't take this slowly, and by God did he want it to last.

"David," she half-sighed, half-moaned his name, "Touch me."

"Shh." He kissed her, possessing her mouth more roughly now, unable to resist nipping her lips with his teeth. "I want to take my time with you."

Her moans were reckless now, and she squirmed under his body. He raised himself up on one knee and she gripped at his T-shirt, pulling it from the waist of his jeans. He took a moment to strip it off, and was rewarded as her fingers stroked his chest and stomach, then moved to attempt to open his pants' button. He grinned and chased her away. He wanted to open her and taste her. If he stripped off totally now, there'd be no time for that. His jeans were the last barrier, and he was keeping them on until the last moment.

He hesitated again. There was more than one kind of danger possible. Only yesterday he wondered if she was losing her mind, hallucinating about wolves and even imagining herself to be one. That she'd broken down and might be a danger to herself, like Sharon. He'd been wrong. But she could still be hurt from it all, and hurting her further would kill him. Then her hands pulled at him again and he was undone.

Her heart was going to pound its way out of her chest. She'd never felt such intense need. The months of stress and the recent bout of danger, combined with David's scent, his kisses, and the touch of his skin did things to her that no single romantic night had ever achieved—she was ravenous with desire. David's hands and kisses flowed over her body, bringing wave after wave of glorious sensation.

She could hear her own guttural moans and growls, and a part of her was amazed at her level of total involvement. His soft groans were thrilling, pushing her level of desperation as he moved so slowly to explore her most sensitive areas. The fact that he wanted to take his time with her was exciting, and maddening.

"Please," she whimpered. His palm massaged her mound.

"Mmmm," he murmured, his lips pressed against her navel.

The seconds as he dragged his mouth downward lasted forever. Within moments she was lost in a spiral of bliss. Her mouth shaped the words, and she breathed out his name.

Finally his weight settled upon her as he levered himself up to stretch along the length of her body. The rough texture of his jeans was breathtaking after the velvet heat of his tongue. She clutched him to her, wrapping herself around his body. She reached again for his jeans and he shifted to allow her hands entry, even as he teased her breasts with his hands and ravished her neck and shoulders with his mouth.

"Just a minute, baby," he whispered.

It was agony to feel him move away from her, see him lift his body from the bed. When he bent to pull off his boots she allowed herself a grin of pure, wolfish satisfaction. He was in her bed, and she was keeping him there. He stripped off his jeans, and her grin widened when as she watched his briefs follow suit. He was wonderful, all over.

"I've got protection," he told her, his voice serious, but his hazel eyes twinkling in laughter.

"Well, thank God for that, and get back here," she mock-growled at him.

He knelt on the mattress, his stiff member proving to her that he needed her as much as she needed him. She reached out to stroke him, rose to touch her lips to him, but he pulled at her shoulders. "I don't think I can take that, and live to follow through," he rasped. His eyes were clouded with lust.

He lifted her to her knees, and pressed their bodies together even as his lips met hers. She tasted her own salty sweetness and his distinct masculine flavor as she opened her mouth to his. Skin against skin, they kissed.

They fit together. He drew his fingers again to her mound and stirred her female core to greater heights. Her heart thundered and she growled for real. He pushed between her legs with his hips, and parted her. His penetration was more than she'd bargained for, and as she gasped with pleasure, he groaned her name out loud. Her climax was immediate; his took a blessedly long time.

For the next hour, time stood still as they brought each other over the edge again. Sometime after that, Helen found herself drifting off to sleep, nestled in his arms.

9

She breathed deeply in her sleep, looking like any other beautiful woman might after sex—a glow to her skin and her hair a complete mess, though he'd never tell her that. But she wasn't like any other woman. Not at all, and it blew him away.

Did he feel any different about a woman who could shift into a huge, dangerous, and gorgeous wolf? Was he a little twisted somehow? He considered that. Nope. The wolf was scary for sure but it was the woman he wanted.

He rolled onto his back and stared at the ceiling. They'd been in bed since early morning and now it was close to noon. Leaving her alone seemed like the wrong thing to do, but he had to wrap his head around everything. He slid out of bed carefully, leaving her wrapped in the warm flannel sheets and heavy comforter so she wouldn't miss his heat. He snagged his pants from where they'd hit the floor and his long-sleeved T-shirt. Hard to say where his socks had ended up and he didn't want to wake her by looking for them. He walked into the hallway before pulling on the jeans and shirt.

He put on a small kettle to boil and spooned a bit of

instant coffee into his father's favorite mug. A little chipped, it seemed to be a perfect fit for his hand, when it had always seemed too big before. He ran a thumb over the chip.

What he been thinking, planning on knocking this place down for some sort of spa hideaway for rich brats with too much time and too much stress? This place had been his father's retreat. His haven. Odd that Helen had thought it would be one for her, too. Having second thoughts after sex wasn't cool. He glanced at the bedroom door. Not that he regretted being with her, not for a second. She was amazing, fantastic, and while she wasn't his usual type, she drew him in and made him want her bad enough that his cock stood up a little, offering to try its best at round four.

Maybe though, she should have thought about what the sex meant to her before he forgot about thinking at all. She had problems he couldn't have imagined before last night. How could he possibly help her with them? She'd been cursed and now was being hunted. Was it even the same people who'd made her into a werewolf? If it was them, why were they after her now, months later? Why curse her and then attack her?

The kettle boiled and he poured it over the instant granules. Helen hadn't stirred. There was no question he was going to help her. She needed him and he needed to feel needed. He'd been to a therapist. He was all too aware that the world's problems—and not even every gorgeous woman's problems—were not on his shoulders. She wasn't even exactly human, although that was pretty hard to believe when he'd just had the most fantastic sex with her.

He took a long sip of coffee, not exactly savoring the instant formula, but tasting the familiarity of it. How many times had he shared a silent cup of coffee with his father? John Sherman would have been amazed at Helen's transformation, but it wouldn't have frightened him. He'd believed everything under the sky was created by a power far greater than him, and that, *"There are more things on heaven and earth, Horatio..."* a quote he'd regularly use and mangle as he chose to indicate his belief in the legends of the local Native Americans. Somewhere, he'd claimed, they had Native blood in their tree, though David had never found it in any record.

What would his father do in a mess like this? Help her. Hold her. Probably keep her. David smiled. Exactly what he was going to do. What they'd shared had been physically intimate, but Helen was smart, strong, powerful in her own way, and exactly what he wanted for far more than a short sexual fling.

They just had to solve a few problems first.

He needed a plan. And within his overall plan for Helen, he needed a plan to get rid of the people who were after her, and get rid of a curse. No big deal.

He settled with his coffee and his phone on the couch and began a search. Werewolves in the United States. Rom and magic and curses.

A long search later and he had an idea about where the Rom wandered on their migration. It was actually a two year long meandering path that touched base in a number of free camping spots as it wound from the east coast to the south and down to Mexico, and then back through the middle of the United States and east again. He'd found a blog by a young woman who was a fringe member of the Rom.

"Find anything interesting?" Helen spoke from beside him and he jumped. The woman was silent as she moved. And, a bit disappointingly, she was dressed, and looked fresh, her hair brushed and no longer mussed from their roll in bed. He doubted he could say the same for himself.

"I found a blog by a Romany girl that I think will help us follow them."

She walked to the kitchen counter where her camp stove

sat and flipped it on. Watching could become an easy obsession. Had she always been this graceful when she moved or was this part of the shift as well?

"The Romily? I saw that one too, but I didn't have much time to look through it. Seemed like a lot about which boy the writer liked best."

He pointed to a cupboard. "Tea is up there in a cookie can. The blog is definitely written by a teenage girl, and there's a lot to sort through. But she does mention the names of places and it isn't hard to work out dates, so I think we can put together an idea of their route. If we follow that, we'll eventually catch up. Then we can find the woman who cursed you and get her to take it off."

She said nothing, stood watching the stove and waiting for the water to boil.

"You do want them to take it off, right? You said you did."

She looked up at him. "I do. But you said 'we' and I am not sure you should come."

He set the phone down on the counter. "You can't do this alone."

"But why should you come with me? Why get involved? You saw what happened last night. Those guys—those wolves—attacked us. Next time it could be a lot worse. I don't even know who they were, or why they want to hurt me, but they do. Not to mention they have fangs and claws, and have some sort of magic. Why drag yourself into all this?"

He stepped closer. "Because you need me."

She sucked in a breath. "And who appointed you my keeper? You followed me up here. I didn't ask you to, and just because we had sex doesn't mean I am going to follow you around like a helpless puppy. For all I know, getting a stranger involved is exactly what brought on the attack. You can't even defend yourself against them. They could come at us as wolves or humans." Anger flared in those fantastic, golden eyes. Very nice. But she clearly had some issues surrounding her independence. If trying to imply he was weak was her go-to defense, she must have had an interesting childhood.

"I can hold my own, and I want to help. It isn't because of the sex. I've had you, and I want you again, but I'd still want to help if we didn't just have fantastic sex."

She pressed her lips together hard and her nostrils flared slightly. Yep, she was pissed. But maybe, considering the rosy color of her cheeks, a little interested in the fact he already wanted her again. Reading her was like reading a book. He'd always been good at understanding people through their body language, but she laid it all out for him as clearly as if she stated her emotions as they changed. It was a hard battle to keep the smile from his face; she'd never get his happiness over that. No woman wanted to be understood.

"If this is about the developments, I don't know if I'm going to still have a job when I go back to Multoma. Helping me doesn't mean I can help you with them."

He rubbed a hand over his jaw. Maybe he didn't understand her after all. "This isn't about work. That can all wait. I'm not even sure about the resort here anyway. And the land will still be there when we sort this out."

"They could hurt you. Hell, they could kill you! I don't even know what they want!"

He reached for her, pulled her in for a hug. She resisted at first, her body still and unyielding, but he held on and she eventually softened. "This is such a bad idea."

He smiled into her hair. It really was a bad idea. But she felt so right. And no way was he leaving her, wolf powers or not, on her own.

The man was an idiot. Well, not an idiot. He was intelligent enough to make her sit up and take notice in a good way. Intelligence was the sexiest thing in the world. But he had to be crazy to get involved in her mess. They sat at the small table, a large map spread across the surface. David has his phone out and they were reviewing the blog, finding any references to the Rom's route and marking them in red on the map. He'd been right about that; amid the fluff of teen angst, boys, clothes, and more boys, there were notes about where bands of the people—that's what the Rom called themselves indirectly, the people—stopped for short periods of time and camped, making money by trading with locals, dropping off handmade items to art galleries and gift stores, and even providing special ingredients and formulated oils to naturopaths.

The insight into the life of the Rom was fascinating. Apparently talking to outsiders about the bands was against the rules, but no one seemed to have noticed this blog and teenagers were teenagers wherever they came from, all willing to bend the rules as they interpreted them.

"Okay, here's where they stopped last." David marked a spot named Woodberry Forest, near Charlottesville in Virginia. "They kind of take a circular route here. Then they'll head further south. Our author likes it when they go to the warmer states and the beaches on the coast." He grinned at her and warmth spread through her chest.

The low, grumbling growl caught them both by surprise. She bolted upright and then laughed. "Guess I'm a little hungry."

He chuckled. "For a minute there I thought the wolves were coming."

She lost her smile. "They are. What time is it?" They'd already had a late lunch from more of her stash and his dehydrated food.

"Wow, it's nearly six."

She stood and paced away from him. She sucked in a deep breath. "No wonder they didn't attack us today. Tonight's the full moon. They need to run. I need to run."

He nodded, his face serious. Their companionable afternoon was gone. "I'm going to make some dinner. When do you…"

"I'll have to go when it's fully dark. I can't be in here when I change, David."

He walked into the kitchen, his movements a little slower than they'd been at lunch, and she scented a light, acrid smell of fear. She dropped her chin to her chest, looked at the floor. Despite what he'd offered, what he'd claimed, that he was there because he wanted to be, and because she needed him, he was afraid of her.

But he turned on the stove and walked back to her, and put his hands on her shoulders. "Do you think they'll be in the woods, waiting for you? I don't think you should go alone. I want to be there when you shift. What if they attacked then, when you were in the middle of it? How long does it take?"

He wasn't afraid of her. He was afraid *for* her. Sensation washed through her chest, like she was being squeezed. He throat tightened. She barely knew him…okay; she did know him a little now. He was smart, strong, caring and great in bed. Hell. He was brave.

Don't believe for a minute you can rely on anyone but yourself, Helen. That's nothing but a lie that a man will tell you before they disappoint you or turn on you.

Her father's advice was never wrong. At least it had never been wrong yet, cold and cruel as it often was. Why would this be any different? How often had he told her she was better off alone, in not so many words? And sometimes, she'd wondered if everyone else was better off without her.

"Don't go there, Helen, wherever it is that you're going. I can see the wheels turning. I am not leaving and I want to be there for you tonight."

"I don't want you to see." Her change had to look repulsive. She hadn't seen it herself, but what else could it be but horrifying? Her bones broke, lengthened and shortened, her muscles and ligaments writhed inside skin that sprouted waves of fur. She became an animal. Why would any man, especially a lover, want to see that? He'd never sleep with her again, knowing what the curse brought out of her.

"I need to know."

She sighed and looked into his eyes. He did need to know if she couldn't convince him to leave her and her disaster of a life alone. Maybe having him see her change would be enough to send him screaming into the night, down the mountain and back home, and far away from her.

He'd be safer that way.

And she'd rely on herself, as always.

"Okay. But I have to change outside. I can't stand it when I'm inside."

"Will you know me after you shift?" They'd had their supper, a quiet affair to be sure, and now they stood in the tall grass. She was naked and wrapped in the car blanket once again, and he stood stiffly beside her SUV with his shotgun braced in the crook of his arm. Darkness spread through the woods, though she could see him clearly in the moonlight. Now that she'd been with him she could appreciate his physique even more—those fantastic shoulders and the deeply muscled chest especially.

The ability to hold back the change slipped through her control and she didn't answer, couldn't. She turned away from him. The last thing she wanted to see was the revulsion that would fill his expression when he watched her give in to the curse. Become a beast, whether he called her that or not.

She let go and pushed instead, calling the change to her in a way she never had before. Not letting it happen like last night, but drawing it in with each breath, willing it to go faster, to make this experience less gruesome for David and less mortifying for her. She hunched down under the blanket and hid what she could, especially as the bones in her face contorted. Power slammed into her and she gasped for breath, shaking as she absorbed the force of what made her a wolf. Pushing might not have been the best idea. No time to absorb the energy, to release the pain. Fur rushed over her body and she lifted her head and screamed, the sound morphing as she was, changing into a long, wailing howl.

The last of her fur and the length of her tail emerged and the blanket slid from her back. She howled again, this time the undulating cry that filled her with a triumph she couldn't explain if she had been in human form. She was wolf.

David sucked in a long breath behind her and she looked at the human male. Still attractive. Still strong, a good mate. He gazed back at her with awe, as he should; she was strong, powerful, and worthy.

The woods called, with their shadows and sounds and scents, begging her to run and hunt. She tasted the air and found no scent of the intruders to her new territory. She let her tongue loll out in a wolf grin and gave in to the call, bunching her muscles and pressing into the loping run that could devour the mountain if she so chose. She ran.

"Well, shit." He was a complete idiot. How was he going to protect her if he couldn't even follow her? Helen in wolf form hadn't looked back once as she dashed off into the woods. He ran but she was long gone before he even hit the edge of the trees. He stopped and looked into the dark shadows. No doubt she could see just fine in there, but him? Not so much.

The only thing he could do was go sit on the porch and try to listen in case she called for him or if she tried to make a run back to safety. He walked back to the cabin and parked his butt on the warped wooden stairs. "Fuck. Goddammit." All he could manage was a curse word or two. "Completely useless, Sherman."

He needed a minute off his feet anyway. And time to wrap his mind around the sight of Helen shifting forms. Jesus, she'd changed so fast he had to think about it all to try to see it. Considering what she'd told him before, tonight wasn't an ordinary shift. She must have tried to hide it from him. He set the gun across his lap and rubbed his face. Last night she'd been gone until sometime around midnight. All he could do was wait.

It was a lot earlier than midnight when the first strange sounds caught his attention. A rustle in the trees, a snap of twigs. In the moonlight he caught movement in the light bush. He picked up the gun and lifted it silently to his shoulder. There was motion in a few areas. Someone was out there and wanted him to know it. He picked up the powerful hunting flashlight beside him. His dad didn't believe in jacking deer—freezing them at night in the beam of the powerful light—but he had one or two of the massive lights for some reason, and David had gone to get one not long after he'd first sat down to wait.

The beam caught the reflection of eyes, three sets. Wolves, considering the height from the ground and the growling that came as he pinpointed them. Likely the same wolves that had gone after Helen the night before. She'd thought there were three and this confirmed it. At least they were here, watching him, not out in the forest, chasing her.

He set the flashlight down on the step beside him and stood. The gun might not be much help against three, it was only a lightweight shotgun meant for bird hunting, but it would sting like hell. If he shot them, they might leave. Or they might attack. He took a slow, deep breath. Then another. A line a cold sweat dripped down the back of his neck and he ground his teeth against the feeling, and the fear that hung low in his belly.

In the next moment, they were gone. No rustles, no twigs snapping this time. Just a sense they'd left. He lifted the flashlight and scanned the edge of the trees, the bushes. Nothing. But no sounds of life from the forest either, not a breath of wind, an owl cry, nothing.

Minutes passed and he eventually sat back own. They were gone. They'd left a message, maybe, that they could have attacked him while she was running. Could have attacked her, too. Their behavior shone a strange light on the previous night. Had they meant to kill when they'd rammed the Jeep at him and Helen? They'd been chased, but neither of them ended up hurt. And they probably could have been— a fledgling werewolf and simple human man. Something he would discuss with Helen when she returned.

A chill ran through him. Maybe she wasn't going to return. Maybe they'd killed her and had shown up to threaten him after doing it. Tell him silently to go away, stay out of their business or he'd end up dead, too.

He paced the length of the porch and caught the edge of his sneaker on a broken bit of board. This place really needed some work if he were going to start using it again. If he didn't knock it down and build a retreat. His father would have both been proud of that, as something his son built, and hated it, as it was on his precious mountain.

David shook his head and looked out into the dark. It was going to be a long night, with nothing but memories for company and worry for a woman who wasn't quite human.

The bitter, angry scent of the intruders bit at her nose the closer she came to the cabin. Not daring to increase her pace, she crept closer. When she was nearly in sight of the small building she realized that the scents had split into three— three wolves—and that there was a fresher path of their stink leaving the bushes near the cabin than the one arriving. Whatever they'd wanted to accomplish, coming here instead of coming after her, they'd done it and moved on.

Her belly tightened. She'd left the man alone when she'd

run. Not her fault; she'd needed the space, the air, the night. But he couldn't keep up and had stayed back. She'd left him undefended. She sniffed at the tracks left by the wolves. No blood. But they could have hurt him in human form. She hesitated. She could leave him now. She knew where to go next, could see it in her mind the route she would take. She could travel a long time in the remainder of the night. Maybe half the distance between her and the closest band of the Rom. The man would only slow her down, as he had the night before, when she'd tried to run from the wolves in human form. Twice he'd shown he couldn't keep up, but… that felt wrong. She couldn't abandon him.

The moon had begun its descent. The intruders were gone from her territory, and if they'd hurt the man before they left, well, she would continue her hunt for the people and if a few throats were torn, so be it.

She trotted into the clearing and spotted the man sitting on the steps. Her man. She walked to him, taking her time. His eyes were wild and his scent tainted with fear. Something had happened, but she could smell no blood. She stopped a few feet from him and waited until he seemed calmer.

"I thought you might be dead," he whispered.

She took a step closer. Not all of his words were clear to her, but the meaning, and the emotion, she understood him well enough. He'd been afraid of the wolves, known they were there, and feared for her.

"They came here and I thought maybe they'd gotten to you and came here to warn me off. To forget what I've seen or they'd be back." His voice was so harsh to her ears, like he had to force the words out.

She put a paw on the step beside him, and leaned against him. He smelled better, the fear fading. He smelled *good.*

Very slowly, tentatively, he touched her. This was also

good. The feeling of his hand on her ruff, the weight of it and the way he ran his fingers through her fur. She stepped aside and he immediately stopped, but she walked to the door and waited for him. He was probably cold. He needed warmth. The fire inside didn't smell good to her, but he would enjoy it. If she didn't go in he might not either. So when he took the hint and opened the door, she trotted inside and flopped down on the wood floor beside the sofa, far enough away from the flames that they didn't bother her eyes or her nose.

"Right. Okay." He followed her inside and locked the door behind him. "Uh, let me know if you want out, okay?"

She showed him her fangs. What did he think she was, a labradoodle? But the bowl of water he offered was very nice. And even better, when he sat down to rest, he sat right beside her where he could touch her. She listened as he told his side of the evening's events. Maybe he didn't think she understood him, not really. But he told her how he felt about losing her, his guilt over not being there to protect her. Then he revealed his fear over the wolves' appearance, and his understanding that they could have attacked him. How he'd waited and not fired. Brave and smart. This man would make a good mate.

The thought occupied her for some time. So long in fact that she barely noticed the man falling asleep, and hardly minded when she realized she was dozing off as well.

Morning came and she stretched. Somehow she'd slept though her change. Slept so deeply she hadn't woken when David apparently moved them to the bed. Her outstretched arm encountered the warmth of his skin and the rough sprinkle of hair on his chest. She took a deep breath of his scent.

"Finally. I wondered if you were going to sleep all day,

Miss Wolf." David's rumbling voice sent a thrill of sensation down her back. She snuggled closer to him and he wrapped his arms around her. His cock stood at attention, apparently waiting for a repeat of the day before. Sounded perfect to her. She rolled over, flipped him onto his back, and climbed onto his lap. He had time to make a gasp of surprise before she slid onto him and began a rhythm that left them panting and pleasured only a few minutes later. Then she kissed him and rolled away laughing before walking to the shower.

Speed had its advantages, but she'd take it slower next time, savor him and let him drive her just a little bit crazy. She stood still under the cold spray. Maybe it was the water temperature, but she was suddenly struck with how completely she'd accepted him in her life. Expected him in it. When had that happened? It had something to do with a conclusion the wolf had come to, but she couldn't remember now. Instead the voice of her father threatened to appear with one of his awful warnings. Put downs disguised as advice. Not what she needed. Today was the first day of the hunt. She had eight weeks to regain her humanity and put her life back together.

She threw on some clothes. It was just about time to hit a laundromat. A few steps in the cozy cabin and she was back in the living room. David stood at the window, his back to the glass and a coffee cup in his hand. Coffee would be so good now. Even the dreadful instant. But the taste was so different now in reality than what her memory claimed. The curse had taken that from her.

"Good morning," she said and walked toward the kitchen.

"I think we already exchanged pleasantries, and definitely had a good morning," he quipped, then pointed to the counter. "There's tea made and the last of the toast. Supplies are running out."

"Then it's a good thing I'm moving on. I'll repay you for the supplies."

"You know I'm coming with you," he stated calmly and took another drink of his coffee.

She picked up her cup, took a sip. "A girl's gotta try. But maybe you should listen to me, David. I can drive you to where you can get some help for your Jeep if you want, or even to a car rental place, but you shouldn't come with me. I have eight weeks off from work to take care of this mess. But you run your company, and you can't just go off on vacation. How will it look?"

He tilted his head and watched her for a moment, long enough to make her fidget under the weight of his gaze. "Since I do own the company, I can go on vacation, and I don't really care what anyone thinks. Do you?"

She set down the cup. "Of course I care. I just made partner. I can't throw that away."

"No, of course not. But do you really care if anyone comments on us? They will. Maybe they'll say it started out business, and maybe they'll say it started out as sex, but they're going to talk about it."

He was right and it made her stomach churn. But it was already done. The gossipers would have a ball with her latest disappearance and David's happening at the same time. It was too much to think about.

"Let's get moving then. We've got a long drive."

He held up her keys. "Already packed except the stove and your clothes."

The Rom's trail was easy enough to find. With the clues from the blog and a little searching on the internet for gift stores where the Rom might sell their wares, David and Helen found two spots where the Romany bands sometimes stopped. None occupied the open fields or old National Park campgrounds as they located them; but they learned a little each time. The bands were made up of five to nine families linked through marriage and often traveling in RVs. They weren't always welcomed as they could be a boisterous bunch, but the nearby towns seemed to have accepted the fact that they would be back, sooner or later. And, despite what seemed like an odd way of life, they made good money through their crafts, and several had a growing business in commissioned art. The expensive RVs proved the point.

David looked at the painting hanging on the wall in the most focal point of the tiny gallery. The price was certainly hefty, but it would look damn good in his office, if Helen didn't mind him buying it.

And wasn't that an interesting turn of thought. She was already starring in all his fantasies; was she about to take over his daydreams of the future, too?

"The Rom that passed through here last night only stayed a day. I guess that's unusual." Helen spoke beside him and he jumped. Second time the wolfgirl had snuck up on him.

She laid her hand on his arm. "Sorry."

Her touch felt good and he returned the favor by wrapping an arm around her shoulders and walking her out the door. "The next town might know more, or we could drive straight through to where we know they tend to meet up and camp at Woodberry Forest."

She let the way back to the SUV and held out her palm for the keys. "Let's just go. It's my turn to drive, though."

He held them out of reach. "Do you think it's a good idea, just driving up to them when we find them and asking for their priestess or whatever to take off the curse?"

She turned away and picked up her pace until she was

half jogging. "What other choice do I have? There has to be some way we can come to an agreement."

He caught her by the hand, made her slow down and look at him. "And if there isn't? If they won't take the curse back or stop the attacks?"

Her eyes filled with tears. "I…I don't know."

They drove for the next two hours quietly. David turned on some music, but neither of them sang along.

"This has to be it." They sat in the car and stared up a long private lane. The cultured stone on the edges of the drive and the gates at the street 'screamed money,' a phrase taken word for word from the blog. "How did they get an agreement to park here for like three weeks every couple of years?"

David shrugged. "Hard to say. The gate's wide open, should we just drive in?"

Helen jiggled her leg up and down and she shifted in her seat. He'd recognized the signs of growing nervousness as they came closer to what was supposed to be a good-sized gathering of the Rom. She'd barely eaten her supper, and the greasy hamburger and fries had for the most part gone out the window to feed the crows.

She twitched again. "I don't know. I mean, there could be a lot of them in there. What if they're all wolves?"

"Could they be? Don't you think someone would have discovered whole bands of werewolves roaming the country every year?"

"Maybe that's why they move around. I need out. I need to run."

The sky had slipped into twilight as they'd sat staring at the estate and he hadn't noticed, but she had. The full moon had been the night before and it pulled at her now to change and run. That's what she needed, not all these decisions and worries. She growled lightly.

"Can you keep it together until we talk to them or do you want to find a place to stay? Go see them in the morning?"

He was so considerate. It made her want to grind her teeth. No, that wasn't right. It was good that he was thinking of her. The wolf inside her was impatient and she needed to gain control. *Soon. I promise we'll go running soon.*

When had she started talking to herself as another person? As two people, or rather one person and one wolf, caught in one body? This was so not good.

"I'm good. Let's talk to them. What's the worst that could happen?" She laughed weakly.

He didn't reply, just put the SUV back in drive and rolled through the gates.

The lane led to a large house, one that looked empty and possibly abandoned, but more importantly they could see a number of RVs parked some distance to the side. David took a small, paved side road and drove close to the first RV.

This was it. Time to demand or beg, depending on their reception, for relief of the curse. Surely, turning someone into a werewolf was overkill for the loss of a camping spot?

He shut the engine down. "Nervous?"

"Oh, yeah. Just a bit." She laughed but it came out a little strangled. He didn't say anything but got out of the car and came around to her side. He opened the door and held out his hand. Taking it gave her strength.

Already, a few people had noticed their arrival and had stopped doing whatever they had been doing. They stood around, apparently waiting to hear what the strangers to their little campsite wanted. Some wore nice clothes, some less nice, some wore artists smocks or aprons covered in paint or other things. All favored bright colors. They didn't seem angry, and Helen couldn't smell any fear coming from the band. A large number of children scampered and played nearby, or were held by curious mothers. Most of the people seemed young, maybe thirty at most. One held up a cell phone and took a picture of the SUV and its occupants.

Helen and David took a few steps away from the vehicle and waited. He didn't let go of her hand. Finally, a young boy with short black hair and a big smile led an old woman to the growing group of watchers. Her back was bent and she had so many wrinkles her eyes were nearly hidden with laugh lines. She wore a long skirt and a tunic, both in vivid shades of purple. She had wispy silver hair and about a dozen bangles on one arm. She stepped forward and smiled at them, raising the un-bangled hand in greeting. "Hello."

This was the Rom? The people who threw blood and curses about willy-nilly? Helen had a hard time associating the people in front of her with the instigators of the events of the last few months. She took the lead and a step forward. "Hello. I'm looking for someone."

"Many people are. Who are you seeking?"

Her words felt like a riddle, or a test. Nothing for it but to tell the truth. "Bianca Donceanu."

The old woman nodded and smiled. "I see." She waved her hand in a dismissive flick at the crowd and they dispersed as if what Helen was looking for wasn't important at all. That, or they did what this sweet old lady told them like she might be the scariest person they knew.

"I am Eva Badi. Come with me and we will have some tea and talk."

Helen looked at David. He shrugged, but they followed

the Rom woman as she wound her way through the gathered RVs until they reached a small one near the far edge of the bunch. She was quick for her age despite a slight limp, and they focused on keeping up. The RVs had been drawn into a rough double circle, all the side doors facing in toward the middle, where a good-sized campfire burned brightly.

"Come in. It's small but cozy." Eva stepped inside and held the RV door open. Unlike most of the other campers, the one they entered was older, and comparatively tiny. It smelled fresh though, like lemon and something…green. Living. A kettle had been left to boil on the two burner stove and it whistled the moment Helen and David took a seat on the built-in benches wrapped around the small table.

Eva set out three cups with silver strainers balanced on the edges. She carefully measured loose tea into the strainers and poured boiling water over the dried leaves. This was the source of the scent that permeated the camper.

"Bianca Donceanu is not someone many seek willingly." Eva took a seat across from them.

"She… We had a disagreement. A legal one over land."

"Ah, you're that one." Eva nodded at her. "Helen Mathews."

Heat touched Helen's cheeks. These people had been talking about her. They likely all knew her secret and all about her the beast inside her. She clenched her fists and tried to stop the incessant jiggling of her left leg. The wolf wanted *out*.

"I did nothing wrong. The city needed another hospital and the land was mostly swamp and owned by the government. There were no legal claims to it."

"But there was a claim. Maybe not legal, but the Rom had an agreement with the government that we could camp there on our travels." She clearly knew exactly what had happened, and what had brought about the curse.

Helen closed her eyes and took a deep breath. "I'm sorry you lost the land, but there was nothing to support your claim. No documentation. And like I said, the city needs the hospital. It'll help thousands of people."

"I have no doubt it will." Eva took her strainer out of the tea and set it aside. "But you took something from us." She filled a teaspoon with sugar and tipped it into the cup. "So we gave you something else."

"You cursed me," Helen hissed. David grabbed her hand, clearly sensing the strain she felt and the anger. Eva merely gave a half smile and nodded.

"There are some who wouldn't consider what was done a curse. There are some who would say it was a gift and that you didn't deserve it. Either way, Bianca Donceanu is not here. She rides with her band. We have no magic here, just a few families with a little of the old blood, and me."

"Ah!" Helen stood abruptly and growled. Her nails were already changing and she welcomed it. Maybe the wolf could get this old woman to talk, to tell her the truth and take the curse away.

David stood too. "I'm sorry, we need to go."

Eva pursed her lips and nodded. "She needs to go. But you should stay. This RV is for guests. I thought, so close to the moon time, you might need a safe place to stay. The band welcomes you…" She raised her eyebrows in question.

"David Sherman," he filled in for her.

"David. We welcome you and Miss Mathews, as long as you keep the peace."

That was quite enough. They weren't going to help her and now David was cozying up to the old Gypsy. Helen yanked open the door and strode out. Darkness had fallen. She headed away from the people, away from the fire and out into the shadows. She needed to run.

David sighed. Eva was more than pleasant, and she'd introduced him to a few of the men and women in the camp. But she wasn't the woman he was waiting for, again. Seemed like he was always waiting for Helen. And she was always leaving him behind. He couldn't even chase her, not on two feet rather than four. At least she hadn't run as long this time, returning after only a couple of hours.

He took a seat around the campfire with a plate of food in hand. Something called *bokoli*—thick pancakes stuffed with meat. They ate often like this apparently, sharing meals in a buffet format and singing and dancing around the fire as long as the weather permitted. Not a bad life.

"Always, the Rom have been hunted." Eva's rich voice came from nearby and as she spoke the music died away. "There have always been the people, and the people have always wanted freedom. We travel, and those who do not understand us, they hunt us." People called out their agreement from around the fire. This story had been told before, that part was easy to tell, but David understood it was being repeated tonight for his benefit, and for Helen's.

He'd seen her glowing eyes shining from where she'd crept under the guest camper after her run. She was listening too, although he wasn't really sure how much she understood. Enough, perhaps, that she might get a better understanding about the Rom, and that would help them in the long run. In the mean time, he'd listen for her.

"In the old country, we made music and art and healing potions. Much as we do now." Eva nodded at various members of the band and they nodded back. "Sometimes, we added a little magic to our creations. This was our downfall."

David put his plate down. Magic. Now they were getting somewhere.

"In our pride we flaunted our talent and magic, building masterpieces of art and architecture in our houses, and we came to the attention of the evil one, Vlad, prince and murderer. He hungered for nothing but power and blood. And once he found us he picked us off, one by one, until the first grandmother made the choice.

"Why do we wander?" Eva addressed the little ones who had gathered at her feet.

"Because we have wandering feet!" piped one small girl.

"Indeed we do. But we wander because of the choice that was made. To never be pinned to a home where evil could trap us. We left our houses, our beautiful homes, that very night. We went by foot, by carriage and by wagon. And so we were saved. And our magic became the path we followed. And when the wars came to our land again, we moved the path and left the old country, and sailed to America."

"They hated us in the old place," the little girl claimed.

"Sometimes people don't like us here, either." A teenage boy said, his voice breaking. David followed the voice and spotted a young man staring at him.

Eva waved her arms and brought all eyes back to her. "In every band there is a grandmother to carry the ways and light the path. I have sensed the path will shift soon and passed this on to the other bands."

Muttering broke out among the adults.

One woman stepped forward. "But Grandmother Eva, I just got that deal at Castaway Art. We could sell a lot there."

They seemed to have forgotten David's presence, but the teen boy refused to let it go. "Are we leaving because of him? *Ruv* Danior says the woman stole our land."

Eva shook her head. "Vano, I told the story tonight of the first path because you and others seem to have forgotten where our magic lays. There would be no *ruva* if we worried about any one piece of land."

The woman who had worried about her art deal spoke again, "Then why did Grandmother Donceanu fight for the marsh camping ground?"

"The path was set at that time. Now it shifts. Perhaps the path stayed long enough to bring Miss Mathews to us." She looked at David and the rest of the band followed suit. Not all the faced turned toward him were upset, but many were.

He swallowed and stood. "I think it's time for me to say goodnight. Thank you for dinner. And the place to stay."

"You and the ruva should go," the boy shouted at him but was quickly hushed by several others.

Eva stood. "David Sherman and Helen Mathews have been welcomed."

A murmur of agreement passed through the crowd. Even the boy nodded and looked away, apparently ashamed.

"Thank you," David said quietly to Eva, "we'll go in the morning."

She nodded. "Before you go I will have another cup of tea with you."

David held the door open and Helen leaped inside. She'd watched the evening's events unfold carefully, but wasn't sure if she'd caught everything. It seemed she could understand body language on a much deeper level but the nuances of tone and language left her in wolf form. She trotted into the tiny bathroom and nosed the door shut so she could change in private.

He'd had a good meal; she'd hate to make him lose it if she changed forms in front of him.

Unfortunately, the change left her naked again. "David? I'm sorry, but would you mind grabbing my clothes from the SUV?"

"I already did, this evening while you were off sulking." There was a thud, which she assumed was her bag hitting the bathroom door. Great, she'd pissed him off. Rightfully so, considering she'd left him with a bunch of possibly hostile people, people who were her problem, not his.

She opened the door slightly but couldn't see him. The bag was there though so she reached out and grabbed it. There was still fresh underwear, although everything else had been worn at least once. A few minutes later she walked out of the bathroom dressed and found David stretched out fully clothed on the double bed at the back of the camper, one arm thrown over his eyes.

She cleared her throat. "I'm sorry. I shouldn't have left you here with these people. I… I couldn't help it."

"*These people* were very nice to me."

She sighed. "I know. I don't really understand why they cursed me like this, if Eva is any indication of the way the other Rom behave."

He reached out a hand and she put hers in it. When he pulled gently, it was easy to sit, to be near him and take in the simple fact that she enjoyed his company, very much.

"Did you hear their story about why they travel around?" he asked.

She nodded. "It explains why they were so mad at the loss of the camping spot. It messed with their magic as well as their way of life."

"Yeah. And I think that kid, the mouthy boy, knows some stuff about the wolves."

"Ruva means wolves. Ruv is a single wolf." She ran her finger absently over his arm, felt the strong muscles under her long-sleeved T-shirt.

"I figured." He pulled her down for a kiss and whispered against her lips, "Mystery solving done for the night. Be with me."

. . .

Light at first, he kissed her until her heart began to pound in a rhythm that matched his. Then he slanted his head and took it deeper, reveling when she returned the pressure.

She opened to him, and he took the opportunity offered, licking her lips and sliding his tongue into her mouth. She tasted dark and delicious, maybe Helen and magic and the night mixed together. He traced his fingers down her arms, then up her sides until he brushed the edge of her breasts. She shivered.

When he cupped her breasts through her T-shirt, they both moaned. She wasn't wearing a bra. He pulled away a bit, enough to leave her lips and look in her eyes. She stared at him, and then leaned in. That was invitation enough. He tilted back onto the bed and brought her with him. The mattress wasn't all that wide or long but it was heaven. She straightened her legs and the last bit of sanity he had fled as her yoga-pant covered heat fit perfectly over him.

If she'd still been naked, he would have taken her immediately and hard. Thank God, she'd dressed after her shift. He had to do this right. They'd be on the road again in the morning, and knowing her, she'd try to push him away again before they approached another band of Rom. It might be their only time for a while, and he wanted—needed—to know he'd given her his best.

He kissed her again, or maybe she kissed him. He took his time tasting her, and she ground against him in response. Going slow was going to take some willpower. He explored her breasts with both hands until she huffed in frustration and pushed him out of the way so she could pull off her T. *Damn*. Her breasts were beautiful, small and perfect and creamy with rosy tips. He leaned up on one elbow and took her breast in his mouth, sucking hard. He palmed the other and kneaded her soft flesh. She moaned in encouragement and ran her hands over his chest to tease his nipples in turn. She pinched one, and he wrapped an arm around her and rolled them both over, so she was underneath him.

He kissed her throat, her collarbone, her breasts. Then slid one hand down the delicate skin of her belly to the edge of her yoga pants. He ran his fingers over the seam of the material from hipbone to hipbone while he circled one of her nipples with his tongue. He drew her deeper into his mouth and slipped his hand down to cup her heat.

She spread her legs wider in response and he smiled at her eagerness. Everything was going fine until she grabbed his cock through his jeans and rubbed. Next thing he knew he was hauling her yoga pants down and pressing his fingers deep inside her. His own pants were down around his calves, and her hands were wrapped around him. He fought for control. Helen had to get the very best of tonight. He slid down between her legs and tasted heaven. She shuddered. Again. And again, and then she arched her back and cried out in release.

A condom. He retrieved a packet from his jeans pocket and tore it open. *Jesus.* He might explode soon. He kicked off the jeans, got on his knees in front of her, and rolled it on. He took a long breath. She was making him lose his mind. He caught her legs in each hand, centered himself and tried to slow his breathing as he pressed inside her.

It took everything he had to take it slow and savor the moment, the intense pleasure of being completely engulfed in her. He set the pace, a slow one, *goddamnit*, and let go of one leg so he could stroke her. Her eyes blanked and she whimpered and shuddered under him. With each thrust in, he circled her clit, until she tried to feebly push his hands away. Instead he picked up the pace and thrust harder, keeping up the circles with his wet thumb against her sensitive flesh.

"David…" She moaned his name, and pleasure wound down through his spine, straight to his balls. "David!" she screamed, stiffening under him in a hard orgasm. He came too, hard enough to make his vision blurry. She was everything he'd ever imagined.

She threw back her head and howled. Not something he'd imagined there. But he'd take it.

1 2

The double bed was entirely too small. David had wrapped himself around her, which meant he was also partially over her. And she needed to pee. Getting untangled was a chore when all she wanted to do was to stay with him, sleep in and maybe have morning sex. Finally, she managed to slip off the bed. He groaned a little, but his eyes stayed closed and she grabbed her yoga pants and T-shirt and headed to the bathroom.

She'd just finished getting cleaned up when a soft tapping at the door caught her attention. Eva. David had mentioned the grandmother—an honorific term that carried a lot of respect but perhaps no family ties—wanted to have tea with them before they left.

Helen flipped the lock on the camper door and waved the elderly lady in. "Good morning."

"Good morning. And how was your run last night, dear?" Eva stepped inside and placed a covered basket on the table. Helen stood back and hid a smile as the tiny woman took charge of the tiny kitchenette and quickly put a kettle to boil. Helen had never had a grandmother that she could remember, and magic and curses aside, this one seemed like the epitome of what she'd imagined family could be. Bossy, knowledgeable, caring.

"I'm so sorry for the way I acted last night—"

Eva waved the comment away and laid out three cups and tea strainers, and the same loose tea as the afternoon before. As she did, Helen caught the slight sounds of David stirring. With a groan he climbed out of bed and staggered a bit to the bathroom. Eva lifted her eyebrows and smiled. The man didn't have a stitch of clothing on. Maybe having family drop by so early in the morning wasn't the best of things after all.

David called from the bathroom. "Helen, was that Eva?"

She had to laugh. "Yes."

"Could you bring me some clothes?"

Eva smiled indulgently and Helen grabbed his pack from the bench and handed it to David when he cracked the door.

"You feel better now that the moon is waning, yes?"

Back to business. "Yes. I really am sorry about running off."

Eva stood and collected the kettle, now boiling and beginning to whistle. She poured the water. "I understand the ways of the ruva, dear. The need to be free. It comes from the magic that makes our path."

"Do you think Ms. Donceanu will take it away? The curse? I really am sorry about the camp. I didn't understand about your people and the land didn't seem to be of any real use. The hospital was perfect there."

Eva studied her for a moment. "Do you really hate the wolf, Helen? Hate the strength, the passion, the freedom that comes with it?"

Helen sucked in a breath. Her heart pounded and she could almost hear the wolf's undulating howl. The one she'd made last night, bidding the moon goodbye. And passion? Was her passion with David simply a bit of the magic? She'd never had the kind of response to a man as she had to him, but was that real? Her heart thumped oddly in her chest.

David opened the door to the bathroom. Thankfully, he'd found jeans and another button-down shirt and wasn't giving Eva another show. Had he heard Eva's question?

"Good morning, Grandmother. Sorry about that."

"It's a morning full of apologies. Not to worry. I still appreciate a good looking man." She patted his arm as he sat and he blushed at her comment.

Eva didn't seem to be waiting for Helen's answer and that was a good thing, because she didn't have one. She lifted her tea strainer from the cup and picked up the tea to blow on the hot contents. The aroma filled the room and seemed to fill her too, soothing and warming her. She closed her eyes and concentrated on the scent and tried to still the ache in her stomach.

Not give up the curse? How could she not give it up? It changed her every month into an animal. David hadn't really seen that, the actual change, she'd sheltered him from it because she could imagine what his expression would be, the horror on his face…

"Helen? You okay?" That same face, filled with concern looked at her now.

"Yeah, sorry." She pulled in a shaky breath, and took a sip of the tea to hide for just a second.

Eva drank some of her tea, clearly unbothered by the heat or by Helen's distraction. "You will find Bianca Donceanu and her band only a few stops ahead on the path, at Blowing Rock on the edge of the Cherokee National Forest, at a large ground where the bands meet. I do not know if she will consider your request. Or if she will listen to you at all. I know she was angry. But the path is changing and more change is to come. She knows this too."

She reached out and touched Helen's hand. "But be careful. As I mentioned before, there are those who value the ability to become the symbol of our freedom. They feel you do not deserve the chance to experience it."

"We've met them." David's voice was deeper than normal, an expression of anger that didn't show on his face.

Eva's lips drew down in a grimace. "Ruv Danior is the leader of that particular pack." She paused, her expression thoughtful. "The wolves help the magic. More magic, more wolves and more wolves, more magic." She stared at Helen. "We need them."

Right. Okay. So maybe Helen had been cursed as a kind of balance because they'd lost the campground? She hadn't answered Eva when the grandmother asked her if she was sure she wanted the curse gone. Maybe she didn't. Or maybe she did, but she wasn't saying either way.

Lots to think about in that very short conversation. What was said, what wasn't.

"Good luck." Eva stood. "Don't worry about the camper. One of the teens will be assigned to clean it. Someone usually needs to be punished for something. She grinned and walked out the door without a goodbye.

"Here's your hat, what's your hurry?" David said sardonically. "Let's go."

But Helen didn't seem to hear him. She drank her tea slowly, clearly lost in thought. He took the time to gather both their things and when he opened the door to take them out to the SUV, she didn't move.

"Sure, sure, shining knight in armor one day, valet the next," he joked to himself. He shook his head when he spotted the teen boy from the campfire the night before, the one with a chip on his shoulder and connections to the wolves that attacked Helen. Maybe he couldn't help her with her internal struggle, not yet, when she wouldn't let him in, but he could help her with this.

"Hey," he said and nodded to the boy while he popped the trunk open.

"You leavin'?" The kid looked around like he was afraid someone would catch him talking to the stranger.

"Looks like it." He threw the bags into the back and slammed the hatch. "Need something?"

"About last night… I know the wolves. They don't like your woman. She's an ingrate. Not happy with her gift. One that she shouldn't have gotten in the first place. Some say the grandmother is slipping, giving her the power when she took away the land. But anyway, they are gonna come after you again, if they get the chance. Maybe you shouldn't go to the gathering."

David leaned against the vehicle. "Why are you warning us when you were so angry last night?"

The boy shifted uneasily, scuffed his sneakers in the dust. "After the fire, they thought I was on their side. I am but… I don't want anyone to get really hurt, you know?"

"Yeah, I know."

"Okay, I gotta go. Be careful or your lady's gonna end up dead, even if she is a wolf. They can't heal from everything." He didn't wait for David to say goodbye, just slipped away between the RVs.

"Interesting." Wolves could be hurt, but not by everything? So they healed well? What hurt them, then? Silver, from the old werewolf shows and what Helen had said about it burning her. Another bit of information to file away.

They could be in real, mortal danger. Time to think about why he was here exactly. He loved a mystery, and this was a doozy, and he wanted to help. But most of all he wanted more time with Helen. She was nothing like Sharon, who needed everything, and eventually needed too much. She was the opposite, never asking for anything, and pushing him away when she thought he was getting too involved.

He'd considered it before, but now was the time to be sure. What did he want from her?

The answer was easy: everything. He wanted to solve the biggest puzzle of all with her: life. Imagining being without her now hurt. Was this what love was like? A choice between pain with her, fighting the wolves and solving the curse, or face the pain of trying to live without her? No choice at all, there.

He walked back up the three steps to the RV door and pulled it open. "Come on, time to go, wolfgirl." He shot her a quick grin at her irritated expression.

Helen sat quietly in the car, watching out the window as the landscape sped by. It seemed David's voice had replaced that of her father. His advice whispered in her ear. *Take it one step at a time. I don't care what anyone thinks. Be with me.*

David spoke into the silence. "Look, I think we need to stop and get a place to have a break. A motel or something."

He hadn't taken his eyes off the road as he spoke and she studied his profile. Was he beginning to regret coming along with her on this crazy trip? It didn't seem real to her, the whole thing and she was the one turning into a wolf, so what did he feel about what they'd discovered?

He glanced at her. "We need to refuel, and I don't mean the car. The blog says that the bands meet at this place for a couple weeks every year, to catch up with each other. So we have the time. We need to think about what we learned and take a bit to think about what to do next. The Rom aren't what I imagined. We need to consider our approach. And we need to do laundry."

There it was again, that word, 'we.' It thrilled her to hear it. He used it a lot and it heated her up inside. A break wouldn't be so bad, with him. And yes, they had a lot to think about.

"Okay. Real food would be good, too."

He looked concerned for a moment. "I haven't seen you eat too much lately."

"Squirrels, mice, rabbits. Best not to think about it too hard."

"Oh." He stared at the road.

Great, she'd grossed him out. She looked down at her lap and the well-worn jeans she had on. How far she'd come from the perfectly dressed woman with the corner office and daddy issues. Working on survival did that. And having someone else to consider for a change.

"Do you need to run tonight?"

"Yes. It's the last night that I have to be the wolf. I can hold it off after this until the moon is nearly full again."

David pulled off the highway and turned into a small town. A few turns later and he was parked at a small motel with a clean-looking front. "That's the first time you called yourself a wolf, rather than a beast. I like it."

Fire burned in her cheeks. Was that true? She'd thought of herself as the wolf lately, even talked to it in her head. Was she becoming comfortable with the curse? Accepting it somehow? Lately, it seemed as though she'd had more control over the change and over herself once she became the wolf. "I guess I'm getting used to it."

"Let's get checked in and find a laundromat and then get some supper."

A good plan. Letting him lead at times was also something she was getting used to. That could be dangerous, if her father had been right about anything. "Why are you with me?" She had to ask. What was this need he had to help all the time? He'd admitted his preoccupation with the urge to help. But why?

He pressed his lips together and stared out the window. His hands gripped the wheel. She waited and finally he turned to her and spoke. "I…was involved with a woman once."

The wolf in her growled a bit, but she stayed quiet.

"My brother always called me a Boy Scout. I was one, but that's not why. I like to help. I talked to a therapist for a while, and I understand I have a sort of compulsion to help. Because I enjoy being needed. Something that comes from being from a big family. But that was after. Sharon needed me. She needed a lot of things. I became what she thought she needed most, what I thought she needed, but I wasn't enough.

"In the end, nothing was enough. She took drugs. She found other men. And then she killed herself. She never got what she really needed, which was professional help. I let her down."

Helen breathed shallowly. She didn't want to smell him when he remembered another woman. Or worse, when he remembered her loss. Was that all she was? A replacement for someone he hadn't been able to help? A charity he felt an urge to aid? A woman in distress?

Asking was out of the question. If she pushed too hard, and she knew she could, she could drive him away. And for once she didn't want that. Didn't want to stand alone just to prove her father wrong. She wanted David. In and out of bed. Definitely in her life. But she wouldn't let him think he'd failed.

"You didn't. She was sick and you were there."

He looked at her, his hazel eyes full of pain. Tiny tired wrinkles edged the corners and marred his forehead. "I know. Like I said, I saw a therapist. Something Sharon refused to do. I'm okay with it now, for the most part."

She laid a hand on his thigh, rubbed.

"You're nothing like her. But I still want to be there for you. You have all this strength, this power in you. You're amazing."

She kissed him then, but a little part of her wondered what would happen when her problems with the Rom were solved.

Hours later, laundry accomplished and supper devoured, she bounced on the bed a few times and then stood to pace. David concentrated on his cell phone, emailing instructions to his secretary and making excuses to a few people about meetings he was going to miss. He looked up occasionally, checking on her.

God, she liked the way his T-shirt hugged his broad shoulders and thick chest. And although he was seated, she could appreciate the tight line of muscle in his legs. Having another glimpse at his ass would be nice. She paced to the window and looked out for what had to be the fifth time. The moon was taking forever. When the darkness was complete and the moon rose, she'd run.

"Getting antsy? Want to go for a walk? We can find a place that you can change safely. We can take the car to the edge of town. I'll even let you hang your head out the window."

She growled a bit and he laughed.

"Come on." He stood and tucked his phone away into his jeans pocket.

She followed him out into the parking lot and into the SUV. This was probably a bad idea, taking him with her to the woods. What if there were other wolves nearby? The ones who sometimes ran on two feet, the ruva, the ones who hated her for being cursed.

Worse, in a way, he hadn't seen her really change. Not all of it. Not directly. He hadn't liked the thought of her eating mice and rabbits, what would he think when he actually saw her go through the change? Become an animal? No way she could force it to go quickly tonight, the full moon was two days past, so she had to let the change take its own pace. If he came with her, he'd see it all.

She headed for the driver's side. "Maybe I should go by myself."

She opened the door only to have him shut it on her. "You aren't leaving me behind again. I can protect myself. And what if they come while you change? We've been through this before. It's safer for me to be with you."

Twilight was almost past and there were a few people in the parking lot. Not a lot but Helen felt eyes on her. "Fine. But I'm driving." She held out her hand for the keys but he shook his head and went around to the passenger side and climbed in. Smart man. She would have driven off without him if she could. She climbed into the black SUV. It really needed a wash. If she were home she'd never let it get dirty like it was now.

Yet another inane thought. Like a dirty car was important. Truthfully, she didn't even miss her apartment or her life all that much. Maybe her heels. Sneakers and boots were getting old. So were jeans and ponytails. She climbed into the car and held out her hand for the keys. He passed them over and she couldn't resist sticking her tongue out at him.

He grinned. "See? Not so hard to let me in. And you can put that tongue to excellent use tonight."

She laughed. Laughing was easy with him. So was thinking about putting her tongue to use, and letting him use his. He leaned over and kissed her. It would be a short run tonight. Just enough to let her wolf relax.

They reached the edge of town pretty quickly, but it was difficult to find a place where they wouldn't be disturbed. Single houses and farms were spaced just far enough apart they couldn't risk stopping, so they drove for nearly an hour before the found a thicker set of woods.

She pulled into what looked like an old hunting or maybe logging road and parked out of sight of the road. For a moment, she sat and gripped the steering wheel. Finally, she glanced at him. David watched her calmly.

"I don't want you to see me change."

"Why not? I've already seen it once."

He reached for her but she flinched and he stopped. She climbed out of the SUV and he followed suit, then walked over to her side of the vehicle.

"You saw some of it. I was under a blanket. And I forced it so it was fast."

He crossed his arms. "I want to see it." He set his jaw and she sighed. Her stomach hurt. Maybe she was going to end up with an ulcer.

"It's bad, David."

"I can imagine." He reached for her again. She let him rub her arm and then pull her in for a hug.

Her heart pounded as she leaned into his embrace. When had what he thought and felt come to mean so much to her? He could be repulsed by her change. He would be. It was a brutal thing, and while it had become something she no longer feared, it was painful, and ugly.

He unzipped her light jacket and pulled it gently from her shoulders. Slowly, he pulled her long-sleeved T over her head. She hadn't bothered with a bra. She let him guide her and undress her and savored the touch of his fingers as they glided over her skin. Would he want to do this after he'd really seen what happened under the curse?

She stepped out of her boots and pressed her toes into the earth, trying to feel the sense of grounding this action always brought, but she couldn't find her balance, could only focus on his nearness, his scent and his heat. The sounds of the forest, the smells, nothing registered except him. She stepped out of her jeans with his guidance, and finally out of her underwear.

She looked at the ground. The pressure to change throbbed slowly inside her. He lifted her chin with his fingers and laid his lips gently against hers. Soft and warm, he caressed her. Would this be their last kiss?

The call beckoned and she couldn't hold it off any longer. He wanted to know what it was like for her to change. Now he was going to see it.

13

<hr>

Helen stepped away from him. For a second he fought the urge to hold on. Her reluctance to shift forms in front of him had dread curdling his belly. Shit. It was going to be bad.

She let out a low moan and turned to face the moon. Her hands were already changing, the nails black and long. Her body writhed and he fought not to go to her as her moan wavered between the one she made when they were in bed to one he knew marked pain. The fact that it slid back to pleasure wasn't lost on him, but then she fell to the ground. Grinding, crunching sounds took his attention and he fell to his knees as he realized that the noises were her bones breaking and changing length. Her face twisted and the glint of fangs caught the pale moonlight.

Her forehead compressed and her nose and jaw elongated into a muzzle. Claws dug into the earth as she growled and groaned and she shook, trembled violently as a tail erupted, skin and bone forming where there had been none. She lifted her head and uttered a howl. Her hair shifted, not disappearing but whitening and blending deeper and deeper into the fur that sprouted everywhere on her body.

There was no blood. There should have been and the thought wouldn't leave him. With this much agony there should be blood. He sat hard on the dirt beside the car. Her howl turned triumphant and she sang to the moon for a long moment. Then she shook all over and turned to him.

Only her eyes were the same. He'd seen that before, when she was a wolf at the cabin. Her beautiful golden eyes couldn't be mistaken, not by him, for anything other than intelligent and present. She was in there. She took a few tentative steps toward him, and he lifted a shaking hand out to touch her.

She let him stroke her once. Then she was off, running through the woods. He didn't move. Very slowly, he leaned back against the front tire of the SUV. "Fuck."

Maybe she'd been right not to let him see. His stomach churned. Not because what he'd seen was disgusting, but because for the first time he had really experienced the magic of the moment. And her pain. *My God, the pain.* He tilted his head back and looked at the moon. Shifting wasn't some late night TV show. This was real, and it put Helen in agony, and in danger. No wonder she was desperate to stop it.

Gradually, he caught his breath and slowed his heartbeat. He stood and collected the shotgun from the back seat.

The forest talked to her. Not in words, but in the texture of dead leaves under her paws; the scent and taste of prey on the breeze; the sound of a night owl far enough away that she wasn't concerned about it or other predators. That the owl was hunting meant there were no wolves among the trees but her. No other big animals either. She could enjoy the run, run for hours and hours before she grew tired and returned to her human form. The run, her human side admitted, was glorious.

At least she no longer feared the human side of herself, and the human no longer feared the wolf. And she had found them a suitable mate. They would take pleasure in him tonight and maybe there would be pups.

The wolf halted, somewhat disturbed by the pup idea. She welcomed it, yet did not. The silly human side wasn't certain, but the wolf was. She would keep the mate. They would find a den and have pups. Simple as that.

Maybe she wouldn't run so far tonight. Her mate had stayed back at the roadside. He wasn't as strong as her, nor, she suspected, as ruthless. Though she hadn't found any scents marking the territory, this was not their land. And she missed him. He should be running alongside her. There was satisfaction about that idea from both sides.

She would just go a little farther and catch the mouse she could sense under a nearby bush, because, okay, she liked the crunchy little things. She ran on, hunted and snacked and howled. It might be a while until her wolf ran free again.

And that seemed a little sad for both of them.

The man, David, stood guarding their…den? Their car. The words weren't as hard tonight, a surprise and an interesting point. Words were human but she remained a wolf. Standing in the shadows and watching her mate. She waited for him to notice her, but his eyes were weak human eyes and couldn't see her in the darkness despite her light color.

She stepped out from the trees and walked toward him. He startled, but didn't point his gun at her. He knew her. Unafraid of what he would see as she changed, at least not afraid in her wolf form, she began to work backward into her human skin. Since this was the way she had begun life, as human, it hurt less. But there were no surges of power to bring pleasure, either.

David watched it all. And when she was done, he was there to hand her the clothes she'd discarded earlier, folded neatly and warm from the car. What he didn't do was offer her a hand up, or an embrace. Her heart dropped into her stomach as she realized he avoided touching her at all. She'd been so right. This would be the end of them. He'd seen the curse and couldn't get past the physical reality of it.

If he left she would be lost. She did need him. She had to end the curse. A tear slipped from the corner of her eye and she turned away from him so he wouldn't see it. She would lose the wolf or lose him.

Shit. She was crying. She was hiding it, but she was crying. The pain of her return from wolf form must have been even more painful than becoming the beautiful wild creature she'd shown him. What the hell was he supposed to do about her crying?

"Do you want some ibuprofen?"

She shook her head. Crap, he was an idiot. Like what the hell was ibuprofen going to do for broken and then magically healed bones? How long did the pain last? Why didn't he ask her all this stuff before?

"I just want to go to the hotel room and lie down, please."

He nodded, but she wasn't looking at him. She stared out the window as she had on the drive after meeting Grandmother Eva, lost in thought. Why had the old lady asked if Helen was sure she wanted to get rid of the curse? Who would want it if it led to pain like he'd just seen? A tiny voice inside reminded him of what had seemed like pleasure at the beginning of the shift. That had to be wrong.

Going back didn't take as long as going out to the woods. This time he knew where he was going. And if he sped, well, he was a little keyed up by the events of the night. Who could blame him? Soon enough they found their way back to the motel and he'd parked. She kept silent and simply climbed out of the SUV without a word. He followed, and they walked to the door. At least it was on the outside of the building and there was no need to cut through long hallways that could be full of people.

He put his hand on the knob, ready to key it open when she grabbed his hand. He glanced at her and froze. Her eyes were open wide and a snarl curled the corner of her mouth. "Get back. They're here."

The wolves. Did she mean the wolves who'd attacked her and tried to run them down were back and in their room? He didn't wait but dashed back to the car and grabbed the shotgun from the back seat. He headed back but she held up a hand, cautioning him to stand back. She gripped the knob and twisted. He could hear a crack from the door even from where he stood as she broke the lock with a single hand.

The light from inside streamed out into the parking lot. Inside the place was completely trashed. The bed torn apart, the TV smashed, the mirrors and painting dangling in broken bits. Their clothes were strewn across the room, most shredded. But there was no sign of the wolves.

"They're gone." She stepped inside and took a closer look. Her nose wrinkled and even he could smell the strong scent of urine.

He cleared his throat. "Yeah, but they sure left a message. I'd say it was 'go away or else.' Maybe with a bit of 'we fucking hate you,' thrown in," he quipped and she rewarded him with a tiny smile.

"Okay." He couldn't deal with her tears, but he could handle this. He leaned the shotgun against the wall just inside the door. "You think you can look this mess over, see if there's anything we can salvage? We still have the camping gear in the SUV. I'll go and talk to the manager, complain how we were broken into and pay for the mess. No cops."

"Fine."

She looked like she was going to say something more and he waited, but she shook her head. He turned to leave.

"Wait." She walked over to him and gave him a long, long kiss. "Thank you."

"I'll be right back."

She nodded and looked back at the room. He stepped out and headed to the motel office.

David didn't hear her when she followed him out of the room a few minutes later, and he was inside the office when she started the SUV with the spare keys she'd kept in the motel safe along with her purse, one of the few things not destroyed by the wolves. They'd yanked it from the wall and smashed it to the ground, denting it to the point where she had difficulty opening the lock, but she got what she needed.

The wolves could have killed them both if they had found them in the room, or killed David in the woods where she'd chosen to complete her change. And what would she have done with him dead? What would she have to live for? Nothing. No family, no friends and who cared about career. Jesus. All she wanted was him.

Her blood had run cold when she'd smelled them at the motel. Three big males, angry and spoiling for a fight. She'd been right. Just like everything she'd done over the years to prove her father wrong, to prove she was as strong as any man, she had to do this on her own. David couldn't handle her change and he certainly couldn't handle the kind of danger she brought to his door. And he shouldn't have to.

She drove through the night, ignoring the constant buzz of her cell phone. Eventually, she just shut it off. Hopefully he'd take the hint and go home. Even if he somehow got a car in the tiny town she'd left him in, it would take him some time. She would have this resolved, one way or another, before then.

When she reached Blowing Rock, it was nearly ten in the morning. She parked on the side of the road just past the town sign and got out of the SUV. The power and magic in the ground surged up from what the grandmothers called the path. Unlike the weak tingle she'd felt before, the magic here roared, its rush untamed and wild. Google told her she stood on the edge of a series of wild National Parks and forests. The wolf, quiet until now and usually silent between moons, pushed to escape and run free.

She gasped for breath and held on to her control. She couldn't change, not now when there were bound to be wolves nearby, ready to defend their territory. Not to mention Gypsy witches who threw curses. She needed to be able to use her words and convince these people to let her go. To release her from the spell. Then David would be safe and maybe he would be able to accept her again.

She climbed slowly back into the car. Once her feet were on the ground and the door was shut, the power became muted, reduced to a slight rushing sound in the back of her skull. She leaned forward against the steering wheel and shut her eyes. For a while, she focused on breathing. Eventually, she slept.

1 4

Helen awoke with a start. She didn't really have time to decide what had woken her, or even how long she'd been asleep when her door was wrenched open and someone reached inside and grabbed her arm. She didn't have her seatbelt on and they dragged her out of the vehicle despite the attempts she made to cling to the steering wheel and the door. The ground met her face with a sickening thud but she barely had time to accept that before a boot snapped into her side in a vicious kick.

Another kick followed the first, and another. She clawed at her attackers, grateful for the ease in which her wolf claws formed. She slashed a pant leg open and was rewarded with more kicks, enough to leave her writhing in pain on the ground, unable to fight any longer. When she stopped resisting someone grabbed her under the arms and dragged her upright. Vertigo forced her to her knees once again and she retched in the grass and spat blood.

Something cracked her in the back of the head. Despite the bright sunshine, her world went gray. Someone grabbed her wrist and they dragged her to a strange vehicle. The scent of the wolves surrounding her made her want to gag and she growled, only to be met with a backhand across the mouth.

Voices buzzed around her. "Should we take her to Grandmother?"

"Let's just slit her throat and be done with her. That's what she deserves. She's disrupted the path for months."

"No. You heard what Grandmother Donceanu said, if we kill her, her *mulo* will be powerful and haunt us."

Muttered agreement made it clear that no one in the group wanted this. Helen did her best to breath shallowly. No need to draw attention to the fact that she was awake and listening.

"Ruv Danior will know what to do with her."

Someone had the foresight to bring duct tape, and the sadistic bastards wrapped it liberally around her wrists behind her back and around her head, closing her mouth but also catching her hair. The pressed her face-first into the nasty seat covers in the back seat and threw a blanket over her. She did her best to breathe, but it grew more difficult when someone sat on her, laughing as she struggled to push them off.

"You shouldn't have come here, little wolf. And where is your man? Did he run away when he saw how we marked your room?" The person on her back mocked her. This was not how she'd imagined meeting the Donceanu band, but it didn't really surprise her that the vandals from last night were part of the family that cursed her. Were any of these the wolves that had crashed her work party months ago? Or tried to run her off the road?

It wasn't long before they arrived. Helen was unceremoniously dragged from the car by her leg, but at least the caught her up by the shoulders before knocking her unconscious by dropping her on her head. She scanned the area but of course nothing was familiar. Except there were three RVs, similar to the last Romany bands, parked together near an old barn. No one walked nearby and no cars drove on the road. No real surprise there, this was a tiny spec of a town and there were likely more Rom here than locals.

"*Sastipe,* Danior. Look what we've brought you!" One of the men shouted. There were no women. The wolves laughed and dragged Helen closer to the middle RV. "A *puyuria* who just can't stay away from us!"

A big man swung open the door of the RV and cocked his head at them. "Ah, Gypsy groupies. What can you do?" He was handsome enough with a thick head of black hair. He grinned and she caught sight of the white gleam of fangs. "But this is more than a groupie. Hello, Miss Mathews."

One of the wolves beside her caught the edge of the duct tape on the back of her neck and ripped. She shrieked as it pulled hair and skin from her lips. But she wasn't done. They couldn't take her down with a few blows. "Hello, Ruv Danior."

He smiled wider, showing a number of teeth that were definitely too long for a human mouth. "Hello indeed. Come looking for more land to steal? A new dose of magic, perhaps?"

She struggled to stand on her own without the grip of the wolves beside her. They let go at a small gesture from Danior. "I didn't steal any land. You used it, but it wasn't yours. And I didn't know about the path. I didn't understand."

He took the three steps down from the RV with a leap that put him too close to her. "It is far too late for apologies. We suffered from your actions. The ruva especially. We take our magic from the path and the moon. Because of you we had to shift the path. Several members lost the ability to change." He grabbed her by the arm and began to drag her toward the doors of the old gray barn. "And because Grandmother chose to illuminate you in our ways, you stole even more power. You don't deserve the wolf."

He pushed her through the door and she stumbled on the uneven floor inside. Her eyes had just adjusted to the dim light of a fire when the room flooded with light and she blinked. A workshop of sorts had been set up in the corner, a long bench filled with tools and materials she couldn't identify, and what reminded her of a blacksmith forge and anvil but smaller.

"Fire it up." Danior dragged her closer to the bench and then threw her to the cool stone floor. One of the other wolves hurried to the forge and began stacking it with coals from the fireplace.

"I hear you have been spending some time researching the Rom and visiting one of our bands." He didn't wait for an answer, busy with fitting a long pair of gloves over his hands. "You will have realized the talents we have. We are makers. Each of us has a way with a craft. We feel it is a gift from the powers in return for the loss of our land."

Very carefully, he drew a long, thin bar of metal from a chest beside the workbench, then continued his lecture. "For me it is metal smithing." He walked to her and tapped the bar against her pant leg. "My favorite is silver. Ironic, no?"

There was a small hole in her jeans. She'd noticed it when they did the laundry but hadn't been concerned. Holes were the fashion and if it got too bad she'd simply throw them away. Now she wished she'd done that sooner. With a precision that said he might have done this before, he probed that tiny hole, only the size of a bottle cap, with the silver bar.

The moment the metal made contact with her skin, she burned.

Several agonizing moments later, in which she had screamed and begged for him to stop, he stepped away from her. Air came in quick pants between sobs. Danior clearly didn't care if she begged and she vowed not to do it again.

He worked at the bench and her stomach rebelled at what he might be planning on doing next. "Why are you doing this?" Her voice shook. "I didn't mean to hurt you or your people. I just didn't understand."

"And now that you do? Will you give us our land back?" A feminine voice came from the doorway and Helen squinted to make out who was there, silhouetted in the afternoon light.

<hr>

"Christ. I cannot believe she did this." David muttered for probably the tenth time. The old car shook and shuddered underneath him as he continued to push the speed to the maximum. He'd bought it from the guy who owned the motel and he hoped to hell it would make it to Blowing Rock. His hair fell in his face again and he pushed it back. "At least there's been no cops." And he was talking to himself again. "I ought to get a dog. At least then I could say I was talking to someone."

What would having a dog be like with Helen around? Would they fight? Would she be dominant and the dog, his dog, become hers instead? Probably. "Why am I even thinking about this?" He blew past a sign that said 'Blowing Rock 10 miles' and groaned.

The woman was unbelievable. She'd left him behind, again! This was getting ridiculous. She likely thought she was protecting him, rather than ditching him, but being left felt the same either way. They were seriously going to have to work on some trust issues.

Lots of thoughts about the future, but not many about right now. What was he going to do when he got to the town? Look for the Rom and their usual gathering of RV campers and her car. That part was obvious. But what if he couldn't find them? She wasn't answering her phone. He had his gun, but only a few shells. The rest had been in the SUV.

The car shuddered again. "C'mon baby, just get me there." He patted the dashboard and immediately regretted it. The surface with sticky with something he didn't care to analyze.

The exit came up quickly and he almost missed it. He'd already left the main highway and the smaller ones weren't marked as well. The speed limit dropped drastically the moment the sign appeared and he had to put the brake pedal down hard to stay under the limit. The last thing he needed was for some local to pull him over in a car that wasn't properly registered, carrying an unsecured and loaded weapon in the back seat.

The best place he figured the Rom to be gathering was near the river. Google Earth showed several large clearings there. From what he'd seen there weren't a lot of houses. Farms mostly dotted the riverside. The town had a quiet feel, but nothing unnatural, at least that's how it felt to him. More like there weren't many young people here any longer, and the aging population left had somewhere else to be on a sunny afternoon.

Driving at this pace during an emergency, and not being sure where to go was enough to make a person crazy. Finally, he reached the slow-moving river and began to trace its path upstream toward the National Park. On the outskirts of town, he found the Rom gathering. There were nearly three times as many campers and their arrangement was more like a triple set of rings than a large circle. He parked on the side of the gravel road leading to the clearing where the majority of the RVs sat.

Getting out of the car took less bravery than he'd imagined and more energy. Driving all night, with stops only for bathroom breaks and coffee, was certainly taking its toll. But this time he was going to catch up with her. This time he'd be there.

"Excuse me, but I'm looking for someone."

The young woman who had been staring at her cell phone as she walked across the road stopped and stared at him. "Most people are."

This was beginning to feel like déjà vu, only with the younger version of Eva. "She was driving a black SUV and I think she came here to talk to Grandmother Donceanu."

The girl lifted one eyebrow and shook her head. "Outsiders don't talk to grandmother." Her tone was scornful. "And besides, Grandmother Donceanu isn't here." She started to walk away but David grabbed her arm and stopped her.

"Hey, let go!"

"Look, I just need to find—"

"Take your hands off her. Right now." A big man with a broken nose walked closer and stood with his arms crossed, staring at David.

David let go and put his hands up slightly in the air. "Please, I just need to find my... My friend. I'm sure she must be with your grandmother."

The girl looked around at the growing crowd. Her smile said she was enjoying the attention. "He means Grandmother Donceanu."

The crowd stared at him, their faces grim. He wasn't going to get anything from these people. They'd closed ranks and he was on his own. "Can you at least tell me where Ruv Danior is camped?"

Someone in the crowd laughed. "Sure, tell him where the ruva are. See if he likes what he finds there!"

The big man who had come first to the girl's defense grinned and nodded. "Very well. You can find Danior at an old farm down the river about a mile from here." He pointed south. "He and his friends camp there alone."

Great. So, now he knew where the wolves were and if Helen hadn't been able to find the grandmother, she would've gone looking for them. He climbed inside the old car and after a few minutes struggling to get it started, thanked God when it cranked over with a bang. At least he wasn't going to have to walk, especially if he was taking the shotgun with him. Doubtless, if they had seen that, instead of laughing at him the Rom would have been calling the wolves for reinforcements.

"Grandmother Donceanu. Welcome to my work room. It's so nice to see you taking an interest in the ruva." Danior continued his work and gathered more pieces of metal together. He didn't seem disturbed by the grandmother's arrival. In fact, he seemed pleased by it. He set the scraps in a concrete-looking crucible and used long tongs to place it in the forge.

Helen watched the interaction between the two. Danior clearly wanted to punish her more than she'd already been punished by the curse. Maybe he even wanted to kill her. She wasn't sure what the grandmother wanted. She'd cursed her; something that Helen had initially thought was a terrible punishment. But from everything she'd learned about these people, they valued the wolves, they valued freedom, and they valued power. Had the curse been a punishment or an introduction to their world?

"I am always glad to visit, though sometimes it seems I am not wanted among you." Donceanu strode closer until she stood over Helen. "What are you doing, Danior? What is this? Why is she here?"

"Why you'd have to ask her. She came here of her own free will. Even after we warned her not once but twice."

Donceanu looked thoughtfully down at Helen. "Like calls to like, I suppose."

"I didn't come here my own free will." Helen wiggled over enough to show the duct tape on her wrists. "Yes, I drove to the town, but it was to come and see you. When I stopped to rest, they objected me."

Donceanu cocked her head and stared at Helen like she could see through her eyes and into her mind. "You came to see me. What did you want from me?"

A commotion at the door caught Helen's attention but before she could really see what was happening Danior strode around the workbench and picked her up by her shirt. "No! There will be no more bargains," he snarled at the grandmother. "When this woman warped our path you did nothing! Nothing to stop her from taking the land and making it unusable for us." He shook Helen until her teeth clattered. "Oh, no, instead, you rewarded her! You gifted her with the ability to change and run the path on four feet instead of two. You gave her *our* gift."

Donceanu stared calmly at him. "Indeed I did."

David pointed the gun at the two men blocking his way. He could see Helen in the grip of a huge man standing beside a forge and another older woman standing beside them. The man was shouting and shaking Helen like a rag doll.

"Let me in, right now."

The men grinned at him like idiots and one laughed out loud. "You have to be kidding. Just what do you think that little pop gun can do to us?"

"You get out of here now and don't come back."

Crap. He couldn't actually bring himself to shoot them. They were young, barely out of their teens. And he had no idea if the shotgun would actually cause any damage to them or not. Were they wolves? Or just young, with the belief that came from that age that they were invincible?

"I need to talk to the grandmother."

They shook their heads, grins intact.

"That's my girlfriend. I need in there, for God's sake. Let me in!" His heart pounded and he grit his teeth. "Argh!" He twisted his grip on the shotgun, grabbed the barrel and swung it, slamming boy on the left in the head and then rammed the barrel into the gut of the boy on the right. He threw the gun to the floor and charged through them. Hands grabbed at him, but he'd played football in high school and knew how to dodge.

The gathered people at the workbench turned to stare at him. It seemed like he was running in slow motion, trying to get through those last few yards to reach Helen.

"Stop!" The command came from both the grandmother and the man holding Helen at the same time.

"I will handle this, Danior. Put her down."

They locked gazes and David looked from one to the other. Clearly, he and Helen had walked in on a power struggle between the wolves and the woman who ran the Rom. Who held the power to free Helen? Who would they have to convince to let her go and remove the curse? Danior dropped Helen to the floor. At least he'd stopped shaking her.

"Who are you?" There was still beauty in the old woman's face; in the high cheek bones and tall forehead, and her long wavy gray hair.

"Are you Bianca Donceanu? The lawyer?"

She nodded. "And grandmother to all the eastern bands. I will ask again, who are you?"

"I'm with her." He pointed to Helen and was glad to see that she seemed to be recovering from Danior's vicious shaking. "My name is David Sherman and I guess you could say I'm her boyfriend. I'm here to negotiate her release from your magic."

A small smile tilted the corners of the grandmother's lips. "So, you love the woman who took away our path?"

A collective growl sounded from the men in the corners of the barn. David scanned the room but his attention was quickly drawn back to Danior who charged toward him but was stopped by the grandmother's outstretched hand. The wolf glared at him. So, now he knew who was in charge. A vital fact for a negotiator. This was his job and he was good at it.

"I… I love the woman who developed a hospital where there was only marshland. Who didn't know about your people or what that land meant to you."

"But you do love her?"

David's mouth went dry and his heartbeat picked up and rattled in his chest like the old car's engine that had barely gotten him here. He licked his lips and ran a hand over the hair on the back of his neck. Helen stared at him and her mouth hung open. News to her, then. He thought he'd made it clearer than that, although he hadn't said the words. Wonderful. Just the way he'd like her to find out.

"I love her."

"If you love her, then I will ask you this: what will you sacrifice for her? Would you take the gift in her place? And the anger of these men?"

***

"No!" Helen struggled to get up on one knee and finally managed to stand. This could not happen. Her mind swam with the revelation of the last few moments. He loved her. And they were going to convince him, Mr. Boy Scout, to take on the curse to save her. The Rom's gift would really be a curse for him. She was growing used to it; the pain and the strangeness and the freedom, and admittedly the power. But she had seen his face when he watched her change. He'd been revolted and pitied her. If he took the curse he would hate her. He couldn't take it and she had to be rid of it. The only choice was for her to be free of it so they could be together.

She scrambled to think of something to stop this. "Don't do that to him. You can't. He is innocent of all of this."

"He might have been innocent once, but now this man has tied himself to you. Your fate is his."

"This is ridiculous." Danior threw up his hands in the air. "What are you even offering, Grandmother? Would you spread our magic so thin? You've already given the gift away to one outsider. Is this how you hope to protect the bands and strengthen the path? Perhaps, it is time you stepped down."

"Perhaps it is time for you to remember who channels the magic of the path and the moon. Go back to your puttering, Danior. I will handle this."

The wolf growled and Helen spotted the tell-tale shift in his stance that said the big man might be thinking of becoming the Big Bad Wolf and eating the grandmother, just like in Red Riding Hood. But Grandmother Donceanu turned her back on him and Helen couldn't smell any fear from her. Danior hesitated, and then stepped back.

"You haven't answered my question. Will you take her place?"

David staggered closer. "Yes."

Helen jumped between him and the old woman. "No! I'll do anything. I'll find you a new campground! You know I work with land development, I can do it!"

Donceanu ignored her. "If you take the way of the path, you must remain a wolf until the next moon. If you return walk the path on two before the next full moon passes, feet you will lose your ability to change and the ruva may have their way with you and with her."

"No, no!" Helen made a grab for the Rom leader but the wolf behind her, Danior, pounced and threw her back to the ground. He grinned at her, amused either by the opportunity to hurt her or the possibility he would get to kill them both, she wasn't sure.

The choice was his. Take the curse and live as a wolf for a month. That didn't sound so bad, except he knew how hard Helen fought to remain human, and he'd seen for himself the pain she endured to shift forms. A month was a long time to live as an animal. What if they didn't let him shift back? What if he remained a wolf forever?

"I don't think the *gadjo* loves you." Danior picked up a long metal rod from the workbench and stood over Helen. The wolf seemed to be enjoying the chaos in the barn. "Or maybe he isn't as brave as you. How brave are you, Helen Mathews?" He touched her cheek with the metal quickly on one side, then dragged it slower across her other cheek. Helen screamed.

Silver. Burn marks rose quickly on Helen's skin at even this light touch. And she was already hurt; he'd seen her limping, so Danior had already tortured her some time earlier. "Stop, I accept!" He couldn't let her suffer at the hands of that asshole, even if he really needed more time to think about the bargain he'd just made and what it meant.

The Grandmother held up her hands. "Very well." She chanted quickly and withdrew a small vial from her skirt pocket. David grimaced. They'd been played and she'd been expecting them, expecting all this. No way would she go around hanging onto werewolf potion in her pocket. No, she'd used the situation she knew was coming to make Danior submit to her, and she was getting exactly what she planned, an opportunity to change David. Why had she thought this would be the way to go, what revenge did she have on her mind?

Helen would at least be safe for a while. He'd hold his end of the bargain. And maybe she could figure out what to do while he took her place and solve the issue between them and the Rom. A quick idea dawned on him, half formed but he needed to blurt it out while he could. "Helen, use the retreat land."

He blinked as spatters from the grandmother's vial hit his face. And then the pain began. His heart pounded and he cried out as his flesh seemed to catch fire. His hands burned and the bones began to break, or elongate. Categorizing the many points of agony quickly became impossible as his whole body was broken and remade. He hadn't thought to pull off his clothes and they strangled and cut at him as they ripped and he changed.

The worst were his legs, the way they ground inside him. Or at least he thought that until his skull crushed inward and back, leaving him gasping in agony. And then the tail… He howled, baying in pain as the bone and flesh built for his tail and burst forth, and then thousands of prickles rippled through his skin as fur burst forth.

Done. The wolf was free. He took in the scene around him: triumph radiating from the grandmother, anger from the wolves in human form, and horror from Helen. It was that—her expression and body language and scent screamed denial of what he now was—that forced him to answer the call of the night and run and run.

"The people have many paths over the United States. Some bands overlap in their paths, and there are times when several will come together for great meetings. But over the years we have lost many places where we could freely meet in any great numbers."

Donceanu rose and pulled a huge, antique-looking book from a cupboard beside the door. "This shows the path of all the bands, including ours." She placed it reverently and gently on the table, despite its obvious weight.

"No one outside our band has ever seen this book. Or even knows of its existence." She opened the tome and turned the thick pages to the middle, where a map of the eastern and southern states lay spread across the double pages. In strange, shining gold ink ran the path that the Rom were so concerned with, the one that contained, or maybe generated, their magic.

"The map is spelled, something not even the other grand-mothers are aware of. Your new campground has already been added." She pointed it out. "We knew change was coming. The path marked here hadn't glowed for more than three years, not until you agreed a month ago to find us a new meeting place. What you have found will make us stronger than we have been in generations."

Helen leaned back on the bench. "I'm glad it's what you want. I really never meant to hurt your people. And I think you knew that. So why did you do this to me? Why curse me?"

Bianca closed the book and took Helen's hand. "It was not a curse. I think, deep inside, you know this. The wolf is a gift, child. For the change I knew was to come."

"A gift. The most bizarre gift anyone has ever received." Helen huffed out a breath and tried to stay calm. "Yes, I can see where the wolf is a great thing for some of your people. But look what's happened to me and David! I've had to quit my job, he's been gone from his company for a month…I don't even know where he is or if he's been all right. Danior could have been torturing him this whole time!"

"Danior is not what you think. He is a leader of wolves. He does what is best for them. Rest assured he has taken care of your man the best way he knows how. He may be a little power hungry, but the new path will give him more freedom and more power and he will be satisfied until well after I am gone. The new grandmother can worry about him then. Your man will have learned under him and done well."

Helen tilted her head back and groaned. She'd never understand these people. "David isn't my man. I'm sure of that. He was disgusted by the wolf, by the way I changed, so I can only imagine what he feels about me after a month of running on four feet." She stood abruptly and gathered her briefcase. She couldn't do it after all—face David and the emotions that were bound to be involved in meeting him again. God, she could barely talk about him. Her shoulders slumped and she fought to keep it together. "I'll take your word about his wellbeing. I think it's time for me to go. You have your path. He's free to do as he wants."

Bianca's lips thinned. She clearly disapproved, but staying just wasn't an option.

"Very well, although I didn't take you for a coward. You will wear the pendant. At least once a year you will shift and remember what it is to be free. If you do not choose the time, the magic will choose it for you. Perhaps, if you listen to your wolf, you will come to your senses."

Helen ground her teeth together. Nothing like pouring salt in the wound. The Rom were a complex people, and their leaders… Well, she would likely never understand their motivations for what they'd done to her over the last few months. Time to go.

The Grandmother stood and patted Helen's arm. "I would ask you to have another cup of tea, now that we have finished our discussion, but I can see you will not stay for it. Goodbye, Helen Mathews. May your path be strong."

"Goodbye. I hope you do well, but forgive me if I have to say I hope we don't meet again." That was about the end of the civility Helen had left in her.

"Perhaps. Perhaps not."

Helen opened the camper door and let herself out. The cool night air felt good after the close confines of the RV, but as she drew a deep breath in, the sound of wolf song, the long undulating calls to the moon and each other rang through the air. She practically raced to her SUV. Getting to it and getting out of the campground became the most important consideration, pencil skirt and heels be damned. Even the laughter of the Rom families she passed didn't matter.

Apparently, she *was* a coward.

The SUV sat where she'd left it and she threw her brief-case inside with total disregard for the expensive leather. She climbed in and started the car, shrieking when the headlights illuminated the shape of a half dozen large wolves. She slammed the car in reverse and spun out of the parking spot, and pressed the gas pedal to the floor when she got the vehicle turned around and put into drive.

Long hours later, Helen pulled back the covers and sat on the hotel bed. She'd driven past the place where she'd meant to stop, a nice little B&B, and kept going until her body rebelled and she feared she would fall asleep at the wheel. At least the Springhill Suites by Marriot had had room for her and they were comfortable and clean and quiet.

She kicked off her heels, staring for a moment at the scuffs on the expensive leather. Ruined. Her stomach hurt, her heart hurt and her heels were destroyed. A tear slipped down her cheek and she practically slapped it away. She picked up the phone and called down to room service for some Perrier, some Tylenol and some digestive crackers, then walked to the bathroom and stripped. Everything but the pendant came off. That she'd keep, a reminder, always, exactly as the damn Gypsies probably planned. A hot shower was in order and then a long, long sleep.

She stood under the spray and let the heat pour over her. The hotel shampoo and conditioner weren't her style but she couldn't bring herself to be concerned. At least the jasmine body wash helped to ease her muscles. And if she cried in the shower, who would ever know?

Finally she climbed out and dried off and wrapped herself in a bathrobe. A heavy knock at the door reminded her of the room service order and she sighed. She picked up her purse, dug a few dollars from it and opened the door.

David pushed the door the rest of the way open.

Helen gasped and stumbled backward, but he caught her before she could fall. And then the door swung shut and his lips were on hers. His kiss demanded everything from her. And his hands, rough and cold from being outside, ran over her body with an urgency that left her reeling. The money she'd taken to tip room service fell to the floor and she grabbed David's shoulders and hung on.

He wanted her, demanded her silently to submit to his desire. And if that was the direction his feelings had taken, she'd accept it and him. She'd take everything he'd give her. God knew it could be the last time she'd ever see him. If this was their last night, she'd have him any way she could.

He stripped the robe from her and let it fall to the floor. His eyes, still mostly golden from the curse with only a hint of hazel shining through, burned her with the power of his gaze and she flushed with embarrassment and desire. He'd seen her naked of course, but now he raked her over with his eyes and there was no mistaking his intent to take her now, hard, and no mistaking the fact that she wanted him to.

They'd been apart too long and her heart ached. But thought and regret came crashing to a close as he picked her up by the waist and pulled her against him. She wrapped her legs around his body and he strode to the bed, throwing them both down on the mattress. The breath in her lungs rushed out and he barely gave her a moment to catch it before his mouth and hands made her struggle for air again.

He kissed and bit at her lips, then her neck. His hands made quick work of rediscovering her body, stroking her skin and cupping her breasts only to pinch her nipples tightly. Before she could open for him, he was pressing his fingers inside her, and her cry of surprise and need only seemed to fuel his actions. In moments she cried out as the first orgasm shook her body, but he didn't stop. He only growled in a strange combination of satisfaction and anger that made her shiver, and she spread her legs wider for him, offering him anything he wanted to take.

He bit and licked at her body, working his way down her stomach in a way that felt dangerous and wild. She shuddered under him, and smelled his skin, that unique scent of David mixed with a hint of what had to be his wolf. Had he come here immediately after shifting? How had he found her so fast?

"David… David!" She cried out in desire as his mouth found her core and he licked and proved until she spun out of control again and the world seemed to sway out of existence.

And then he was on her, thrusting, taking, and erasing the last bit of thought in her mind. She screamed and he howled as they both rushed over the edge and fell.

David lay on her, pinning her to the bed, and she could feel his heart racing. She licked her lips. Her mouth was dry from panting. She tried to clear her throat. He gripped her like she might be trying to get away. Not a bad idea. Now they'd have to talk. And there was that cowardice again, something her father had accused her of, but nothing had ever made her believe she possessed. Until now.

He rolled off her and laid on his back. They both stared at the ceiling. "I'm sorry." The words came out in unison followed by a long few minutes of silence.

He spoke first. "I was angry at you. I shouldn't have just barged in here. And then, you looked so good. I wanted you so much—"

"You don't have to explain. And you certainly don't have to apologize. I wanted you too." She couldn't look at him. "I know you hate me for what the Rom put you through. The pain and the humiliation of being an animal. Eating God knows what. Subjected to Danior's anger and sadistic leadership. I don't blame you. I saw how repulsed you were when I changed and how you pitied me. I know you probably came here for some closure. You can tell me how much you hate me. I take full responsibility. And when you find out the rest, you're going to hate me more."

"The rest? What did you do, Helen?" He rolled onto his side and stared at her. She could feel his gaze on her face and she closed her eyes.

"I… I gave them the mountain resort. Not all of it. Of course none of the land you bought. I purchased more under it and on the other side of the mountain. They needed a place with so many specific requirements, I couldn't find anything else in the month they gave me. It doesn't mean you can't build what you want there," she said quickly. "Just that it might be smaller, and you'd have some neighbors…but they aren't there all the time and the wolves might actually bring in some tourism—"

"I don't want tourists."

"Oh… Of course you don't. I'm sorry."

"And this? What is this? I felt something from it." He fingered the chain on the wolf pendant."

"Part of the deal. I gave them a place to camp, a way to add to their path, and they freed you, freed both of us really. No being hunted." She sat up, and then stood, her back to him. "The necklace is a reminder. So I don't forget the Rom. At least once a year I have to change and become the wolf. I know you don't want to see that again. I know you don't want me near you long enough to see me as an animal or to remind me of what you've been through, all because you tried to help me."

She turned back to him. God, he was gorgeous. The sheets only covered his hips. But his eyes had turned dark and his lips were pressed tightly together. His hands had bunched into fists. Looking at him was a mistake.

"I'm not angry because you used the land. I told you to do it. I don't even want the retreat there anymore. I fell in love with the old place again when we were there together. And I'm not angry because they brought me to the wolf. Yes, it was painful. Yes, Danior is an asshole, although he saved me more than once and taught me a lot. I'm angry because you left me, damn it! You left me there, in a form I had no idea what to do with, with people I didn't know, and no idea of what happened to you and no way of knowing what you were going to do or what they might do to you.

"I don't hate being a wolf, I love it. Maybe you don't, maybe all you still see is the animal, the beast, but over the last month I have experienced so much… I don't even know if you got to see everything I have. You've never run with a pack…" He fell back on the bed and rubbed his hands over his face. "God, Helen. I don't know where you got the idea that I was repulsed or that I pitied you. I was upset over the amount of pain I saw in you when you changed. And now I know firsthand how the pain is mixed with power and pleasure. I never pitied you." He threw off the sheets and stood. "I never pitied you, I envied you!" Now he was shouting.

Helen froze. She stared at him, a beautiful male god in his anger. He'd put on even more muscle mass during his time in the woods, something she couldn't help notice. She shook as she replayed his words. "You aren't angry at me?"

"Yes, I am, damn it! But for all different reasons." He walked to her, pulled her into his arms, and kissed her. Then he groaned and rested his head on top of hers, the wolf pendant trapped between them. "I'm still angry that you left. That you didn't tell me about how you felt. That I told you I loved you and you ran away."

She listed to his heart beating. "I love you." She pulled away, catching his hands in hers. Slowly, keeping her eyes on him, she led him back to the bed.

"I love you," she repeated herself. "I'm sorry."

"It's just that you scared me," he muttered. He looked into her eyes. "I was afraid you weren't coming back."

Ah. Her heart twisted and she fell so much further. "I was afraid you wouldn't love me anymore after everything. Hearing you say you loved me at Danior's workshop, I convinced myself you only said it so that they would let me go. That you were pulling your Boy Scout routine. The knight in shining armor."

"For you, always. But it was still the truth." He kissed her. The wolf pendant buzzed between them. He leaned back, looked at it again. "The Rom drive a hard bargain. I wonder what it's going to take to get them to make us another one?"

Now she grinned. "Well, I did happen to get a good look at the map of their path. There might be something we can negotiate."

He laughed. "Perfect. C'mon, wolfgirl. Let's try this again. Say it with me. I love you, and I am never leaving."

"I love you. And I am never leaving."

His lips met hers and the exhilaration over the freedom she'd experienced on her first run through the woods as a wolf returned. This time she wouldn't run alone.

EPILOGUE

Pine needles, moldy old leaves, mud, and the scent of something small and furry tickled her nose. She waited, frozen, and he heard the tiny rustle that must have caught her attention. Then she leaped, pounced, and killed. Mouse. Perfect snack, although she'd never admit it to anyone except him. Maybe not even then, although he knew how much she liked them. He grinned at her and she grinned back, her long muzzle filled with teeth and a lolling tongue. Her fur ruffled in the breeze and he walked to her, nudged her with his shoulder. Time to go back.

Running. This was the part he liked best, breaking into the long loping run that ate the distance between them and home.

The cottage was home now, their territory, at least as wolves. There were times when their other forms interfered and they lived elsewhere, in places the wolves didn't care for. Here on the mountain they had the big wooden den, comfortable for both their forms, and the woods to run and hunt.

They had company too, the ruva of the various bands,

should they want it. Right now he didn't. He wanted to take his mate to their den and love her.

Returning home didn't take long tonight. And the shift was easier now for them both. The pain far less now that he'd learned to accept and ease into the change. Soon enough he stood naked with his mate…his wife, just outside the old cabin. He'd renovated it for her. Given her all the bells and whistles, although she claimed she didn't need them. Right now all she seemed to want was him on her, in front of the quiet fire he'd left burning in the big fireplace.

He was happy to oblige.

"God, there is nothing like sex after a run." She sighed and rested her head against his chest.

He pressed a kiss to her forehead. "I know. And I really want to stay another week. But we have to get back." She ran his company with him now. And they had the working campground that paid for the Rom's bigger one on the other side of the mountain. But work wasn't the driving force it had been for either of them. A source of satisfaction, yes. But they had each other as a focus now. And their extended family, the Rom, as well as his parents and brother. And soon…

He slid his hand down her belly, feeling the curve there that held the life they'd made between them. Grandmother Donceanu had assured them the baby would be fine even if they shifted up until the day it was born. Helen seemed determined to try it.

He let himself touch her a little further down, and grinned at her restless movement at his touch. Her mystery, the one that had pulled him to help her, was long solved. Not they had a much bigger one to share. Love and family.

A Note from the Author About The Rom

This book was made completely from my imagination. But the people, and some of their lifestyle and language, are real. I've taken a great deal of liberty with their history and magic—which I imagine they have in bounds—and hope I cause no offense. The Rom currently number as many as one million in America, although that number is difficult to prove as the members of the bands remain in the majority at least partially nomadic. They do travel across the country annually and many hold jobs that involve crafts and skills most city dwellers seem to have forgotten, as well as offer fortune telling and other small magics.

For more information about the Rom, please read this article by Encyclopedia Britannica. https://www.britannica.com/topic/Rom. I have spent a little time reading about their history and their language and names from this and other sources, and used a bit where I could.

Glossary – from source http://www2.arnes.si/~eusmith/Romany/glossary.html

Bokoli – thick pancakes stuffed with meat
Ruv – Wolf
Ruva – Wolves
Mulo – spirit of the dead
Sastipe – greetings
Puyuria – Gypsy followers or groupies
Gadjo – non Rom man

Lilly Cain is a wild woman with a deep throaty laugh, plunging necklines and a great lover of all things sensual – perfume, chocolate, silk! She never has to worry about finding a date or keeping a man in line. She keeps her blond hair long and curly, wears beautiful clothes and loves loud music. Lilly lives her private life in the pages of her books.

All of the above is just so much silliness. When not living up to her pen name, Lilly lives in Atlantic Canada, although she spent eight years in Bermuda, enjoying the heat and the pink sands. She returned to her homeland so she could see the changing of the seasons once again. When not writing

she paints, swills coffee and vodka (but not together), and
fights her writing pals for chocolate (true story).

Lilly is a single mom who loves reading and writing,
dabbling in art and loving and caring for her two daughters.
She loves romance in all of its varying heat levels. She loves
the chilling moments and the humor in her novels as much
as the steaming hot interludes. Her stories are an escape and
a release, and she hopes that they can give you that
power, too.

To contact Lilly and to find out more about her books, reach
out to her website at http://www.lillycain.com

Coming up next? *Dark Redemption* - An all new erotic
vampire/dragon threesome, two men with history and a
woman with attitude. This story will release in serial format
with the first chapters available in April! Check Lilly's
website for dates and links.

DARK REDEMPTION

Having watched his vampire pack leader killed before his eyes, James Drummond is in trouble, big trouble. He is thousands of miles from what is left of the pack where he was once second in command. He's being hunted, possibly by the vampire that destroyed his maker, possibly by something else, something worse. Stumbling into the territory of an ancient dragon doesn't make things better and crossing paths with the one woman he'd turned and the only woman he'd ever loved makes life downright hell. Especially when the first thing she does is try to kill him.

Ava's life is hard. What life she has, that is. Turned into a vampire and abandoned by her maker, she's had to fight for everything she has—even for the understanding she has of herself. She's vowed to kill him for that, even though she'd once loved him. James's arrival simply means she won't have to hunt him down some time in the future. Except somehow he has managed to become a captive of a dragon, something even she might not want to tangle with. That is until she meets the red hot sexy creature and finds herself at the mercy of his sensual flames. Then it's a tossup—kill the vampire or obey the beast.

For Akio, an ancient Japanese dragon-man, James's appearance represents a chance to find meaning in his days once again. He could be Akio's one chance at redemption, a way to make up for the death of a family he'd once protected. All he needs to do is heal the soul-wounded vampire, give him back the life he should have had. He will do it, even if it means giving up a woman that makes Akio feel in ways he hasn't in centuries. If, of course, he can keep James alive. For there is something hunting them…